Spanking Tales

AN EROTIC SHORT STORY ANTHOLOGY

EMILY ROOKS

True Lust

Contents

Curiouser and Curiouser

What would you ask? You know, if you knew almost nothing about sex while your roommate is getting it every day – twice sometimes, I suspected – and then she always told you about it? I mean, I knew the obvious stuff, like how it was done, and certainly I'd had sex, though it was more like awkward fumbling in the dark than what Maryam and Clayton were doing.

"Then he told me to turn over and get on all fours," she said. "When I did, his hands grabbed my butt cheeks and raised them up, and in one quick thrust he was in me. Oh God, that left me dizzy. Then, just as I was getting into a rhythm with him, he *slapped my ass.*"

"Did you like it?" That's what I asked, as I crossed my legs, hoping she hadn't seen the wet spot forming on my pajama bottoms.

Her eyebrows rose. "Like it? *Of course* I liked it, Alison."

Whether she meant she liked being taken from behind or getting spanked, I didn't know. Probably both, I figured. Maryam liked everything Clayton did to her.

And so apparently did I.

That night, when Maryam left for the floor lounge to

1

take a call from her sister studying in Los Angeles, my fingers found their way to between my legs. I imagined Clayton's large hands guiding me to all fours, then as kneeling behind me, he lifted up my butt and rubbed his cock against my slit. The California sun must have caused Maryam's sister's brain to forget the time difference, I thought, and then that's where I found Clayton and me – on a beach framed with palm trees, the ocean surf smacking the shore in rhythm with his cock, as he took me from behind. My breathing grew heavy, as a finger circled my clit beneath the sheets, and my hips gyrated as another finger slipped inside me. My moans grew louder and my heart thudded, then *slap*, his hand struck my ass cheek hard. My hips rose from the mattress, as he slapped the other cheek, and I froze as letting out a deep gasp of pleasure. For a long moment, I floated, as if on a current of warm air, and then my body relaxed and slowly drifted back to the mattress, where I lay panting.

My orgasm came when he slapped my ass, I realized. Did I really want to be spanked too? Me, a mousy little English major who worked at the campus library and knew almost nothing about sex wanted to be spanked? Well, it was just two slaps, I told myself, not an actual spanking.

Exhaustion overtook me, and I wafted off to sleep as dark-haired Clayton, his cum where my fingers had been, held me close in the sand, his strong chin nuzzling my soft neck.

***

As pushing the reshelving cart down the aisle, my knit sneakers squeaking with each step, the title stood out like a flashing red light. Right there, among the thousands of books on the shelves, right there in the HQ79s, was the book "Spanking, Sex and Love." I reached for it then paused. *What if someone sees me?* I stole a glance in both directions, saw no one. I readjusted my glasses so they were lower on my nose then took down the book and opened it to a random page. It read:

"Turn around," your lover whispers in your ear, "and place your hands on your knees. I'm going to spank you."

My pulse quickened. *Is this what really turns me on?*

"Hi Alison."

Clayton. My head snapped up, and the book clapped shut.

"What're you doing?"

I could feel my face reddening. "Um...reshelving."

Clayton's gray eyes scanned the shelves I was standing before, and a sly grin came over his face. "Lucky you."

Our eyes locked, as we smiled at one another.

"I came down here looking for a book," he said.

"Good thing you're not in the Science Building then," I said, trying to be funny, but the moment after saying it realized I sounded sarcastic.

His eyes crinkled, as he grinned. "Yeah, that did sound kind of stupid of me, didn't it?"

Wait, is he nervous too? "Need help finding it?"

"No, it should be right there." He pointed at the shelf

where I'd pulled "Spanking, Sex and Love."

I looked at the empty spot before us. Clayton wanted a book in the HQ79s? Is that where he learned everything he did with Maryam? "Um, let me step aside."

"No worries," he said then scanned the shelf. "Huh, it's not here. Looks like there's a book missing where it should be. The library's computer said it was checked in."

I pressed the book closer to my chest, trying to hide its title with my arms. "Somebody must have taken it but not checked it out yet. I thought I heard someone nosing around over here when I was in the other aisle."

He nodded slowly. "Oh well. I won't need it anytime soon. Maryam is going out of town this weekend."

"Yeah, her dad's birthday party is tomorrow. You're not going with her?"

He shrugged. "She didn't ask me."

That's weird. Maybe she doesn't want her family hearing you fuck her brains out. "I'm sure she'll tell you all about it when she gets back."

He chuckled. "Yeah, that's Maryam, tells every detail. Well, see you around."

I watched his perky butt, as he walked away. *Yeah, I'll see you in tonight's fantasy.*

***

With Maryam gone, I read "Spanking, Sex and Love" late into the night then masturbated, pretending my fingers were Clayton's. Lulled into deep sleep by orgasm, I got up late and missed Saturday breakfast at

4

the dining hall so headed to the coffeeshop just off campus. The Maryland sun shined brightly, and I hoped my thick sweater wouldn't be too warm for April. All during the walk, I couldn't stop thinking about what I'd read in the book...

Spanking is sensory play. Like the lightness of a kiss, the trailing of the lips up a neck, or massaging a back, it often is pleasurable when done gently.

The moment I stepped into the coffeeshop, I spotted Clayton sitting at a table for two. *Get out of here quick!*

He looked up – must have felt my intense stare – and in the same instant smiled and waved me over.

Can't get out of here now! Hands in pockets, I walked over to him.

"Alison! Good to see you again."

Better be, you fucked me last night. I suppressed a giggle. "You too. I slept in."

He nodded. "The grub here is better than at the dining hall anyway. Go grab yourself something and join me."

"Okay." *What am I getting myself into?*

A few minutes later, I came back with a breakfast ciabatta and black coffee.

"Great weather, isn't it?" he said.

"Mm-hmm," I said over my first bite. *Great, talking with my mouth full, I look like a pig.* Finally I finished chewing. "Any plans now that Maryam's out of town?"

He grinned. "Ah, so Maryam has you spying on me!"

I blushed. "No, not at all. I'd never tell Maryam anything."

"That's good. I wouldn't want Maryam to know all of my secrets."

"Your secrets?"

"Like that I go to the library to get ideas for our...*time* together."

"I won't mention a thing about it. Librarian confidentiality."

"That's appreciated. I'd prefer that she thought I was naturally good."

I couldn't resist. "So you think Maryam believes you're good?"

His face blanched, but then he saw the corner of my mouth curving into a smile and laughed. "You had me there for a second."

"Don't worry. Maryam thinks you're good. *Really* good."

His face reddened, as he smiled widely. "I hope she doesn't tell you *everything*."

I took a long breath and quick bit into my ciabatta to avoid answering.

"So she *does* tell you everything."

"How would I know? I mean, I'm not there when you two are doing it."

He sat back, gave me that sexy grin again. "Well, she may tell you everything, but don't judge her. She won't do *everything* with me."

"Who's judging?" *So what do you want to do that Maryam won't?*

"But back to your original question. I don't have any plans for the day."

"Me neither." *Well, just to read that book you wanted to check out.*

"Want to do something together?"

To hell with the book. "Okay."

***

Clayton and I moved on from the llamas at the Calvert Mills Park Zoo, as the spring sun warmed our faces. I'd tied the thick sweater round my waist, and he'd grabbed a soda to stay cool. We walked slowly so his drink wouldn't slosh out of the cup – straws weren't allowed at the zoo – and talked about nothing and anything...classes we were taking, favorite professors, what towns we came from.

"Wanna check out the petting zoo?" he said.

I shrugged. "Why not?"

There wasn't much to see at the zoo; it was one of those small town parks that just happened to have a few animals. Still, it was a scenic place to walk, and who knew what crazy things the animals might do there?

Clayton stuck a quarter into a gumball-like machine, and out poured little beige pellets onto his palm. "Here, take some." He dumped about half of them into my cupped hand.

The instant we stepped inside the caged area, two goats and a lamp scurried over, sniffing our hands. I opened mine, and a wet tongue lick later, one goat had scarfed everything I held.

"Well aren't you greedy?" I said, as Clayton laughed while the other goat and the lamb sniffed, wondering where their helpings were.

Clayton fed them with his pellets. "I'll get some more."

I watched his perky butt, as he walked away then sauntered to the other side of the pen where a small goat stood apart from the others, as if it were a little scared. Kneeling, I spoke softly. "It's okay, I won't hurt you. Come here."

It looked at me and lifted a front leg as if to walk over but then put it down. The poor thing didn't know what it wanted. No, strike that. It knew what it wanted. It just didn't know if it should take the risk of getting it.

Clayton brought over a handful of pellets and dropped them in my palm. I held out that hand toward the timid goat. It took a step toward me.

"Come on, sweetie, it's all right."

A moment later, the shy goat was in front of me, still uncertain if it should take the pellets or not.

"It's okay."

And then the goat stretched its neck and gulped half of the pellets from my palm. With one more sweep of the tongue, it took the rest. Rather than back off, it stood there, trustful.

"You're happier now, aren't you sweetie?" I said.

We fed a couple of more of the goats and lambs, then left, washing our hands at the basin outside the pen. Walking through the zoo together, our hands almost brushing one another, I found myself looking at every butt we passed and thinking about the spanking book. It had said spanking wasn't a sign of some mental condition or trauma. Clayton certainly was a normal guy, and he was interested.

Enjoyment of erotic spanking generally does not stem from childhood spankings used as punishment, the book said. Some men and women, however, find erotic spanking framed as punishment or corrective action enticing.

Yeah, that *did* sound enticing.

I'd always been curious about the shapes of butts and what they felt like. During middle school in the girls' locker room, like all of my other classmates, I'd steal looks at their nude bodies, but I also glanced at their derrières, cataloging all the different kinds – A-shaped, upside down heart, round, square, V. When seeing football players at high school games swat one another on the butt, I thought it kind of sexy. Had Clayton done the same, maybe felt the same, when young?

We stopped in front of the brown bear exhibit, watched it play with a ball on a fake rock terrace.

I turned to Clayton, as he gazed at the bear, a boyish grin on his face. He smelled of vanilla and cedarwood; how had I not noticed this before? "Clayton, I'm having a really nice time with you this afternoon."

He looked at me, and our eyes locked. "Me too," he said softly. Then he slowly leaned toward me and paused, and I began to close the gap, and then, our lips a hair's breadth apart, we each pulled back, blushing.

"Um, should we look at the sika deer?" Clayton said, avoiding my eyes.

"Yeah, okay."

We walked a little farther apart from one another,

though still side by side. I couldn't believe I almost kissed Maryam's boyfriend. *Maybe being with him isn't a good idea.*

Up ahead of us, a guy squeezed his girlfriend's butt then slapped it lightly. I almost got wet right there. They leaned into one another, and for a moment, I wished Clayton and I were that couple.

My whole head was in chaos. I didn't know what I wanted.

Just before we reached the deer exhibit, a hulking guy walked toward us.

"Dante!" Clayton said.

"Clay-man!"

Clayton turned to me. "This is my friend Dante. Dante, this is Alison, Maryam's best friend and roommate."

We nodded at one another, Dante smiling.

"You and Dante have a lot on common," Clayton said.

"Oh, like what?" I said as staring into Clayton's gorgeous gray eyes.

"He helps run the campus law library."

I shrugged. "Cool."

"Dante is single, and with you being single, too, I was thinking maybe you two could go on a double date with Maryam and me sometime. Whadya say?"

My mouth dropped, as Dante stood there looking expectantly. *What the hell, Clayton, we almost kissed, and now you're pawning me off?* My nostrils flared.

I stormed away, lip curled, as Clayton called after me.

***

Back in my dorm room, I'd finally calmed down. I didn't know what overcame me, didn't know that I could get so angry, though it was justified.

Not so justified was me almost making out with Clayton. Okay, we didn't make out, just almost stole a kiss, but that was bad enough.

Despite my anger at Clayton, I couldn't stop thinking about him, about him spanking me. Paging through the book he'd wanted, I marveled at the pictures of paddles, willow switches and riding crops...spanking benches and vaulting bucks...spanking skirts and motorcycle chaps.

Is this is who I am? Maybe the reason my sex life is so boring isn't because I'm a mousy little English major working at a library but because I don't know what I want sexually

What if I got in touch with my sexuality – would I then be happier with who I am?

Hmmm, "curiouser and curiouser" indeed.

I grabbed my Kindle, found an erotic anthology I'd hid deep in my library, and started reading. And then I reached this passage:

Her bottom played out a nervous dance of expectancy. When he brought his palm down hard on her sweet bottom, she gasped with pleasure, relishing the sting in his fingertips, the soft spongy feel of her flesh, and the small yelp she made of acknowledged contact. A red hand print appeared immediately on her already pink cheek, and he struggled with the urge to lean forward and nip the mark with his teeth.

I pulled off my clothes and grabbed my hairbrush from the dresser. Laying tummy down on the bed, I reached back and slapped a butt cheek with the brush. It stung, but the pain quickly dissipated. I smacked myself harder, and though the pain lasted longer, it wasn't enough. *Maybe a lot of quick smacks, over and over.* I tried that, and as my butt heated up, a wet spot formed between my legs. Still, though the sting lingered, it didn't hurt enough, all because I couldn't deliver a hard whack from my angle.

Switching the brush to the other hand, I smacked at the untouched cheek then slipped a hand under my panties and found my clit. It hardened with each strike of the brush and flick of my finger. I groaned into the sheets.

And then there was a knock at the door.

***

Knock, knock.

Eyes wide, I shouted, "Just a minute!"

I quickly threw on my pants and shirt, kicked my bra and panties under the bed, and looked through the keyhole.

Clayton.

I half opened the door.

"Allison, I want to apologize," he said.

"Okay, apology accepted."

"Can I come in?"

For a moment I stood there then opened the door wider, and he stepped past me. His vanilla and cedarwood scent left me a little heady again.

12

"I shouldn't have asked if you would go out with Dante, not after what happened between us this afternoon. I didn't realize that at the time, but I do now."

I went to sit down. His eyes locked onto my calf and the curve of my ass slowly lowering into the desk chair. *Maybe he's feeling the same thing I am, and he's trying to avoid a big mess with Maryam.* "It's okay. I've never really gotten mad like that before. I probably shouldn't have stormed off."

He nodded. "I can understand why. I guess we should talk about what happened...earlier."

What happened earlier. Like it's some unspoken truth that no one can say. "Do you and Maryam talk when things like this happen?"

"Nothing like this has happened to me before. We do talk when we have disagreements. But it's mostly me listening. Getting a word in edgewise with Maryam is difficult to say the least."

We both chuckled.

"I think we should forget about what happened," I said at last. "I don't want to mess up your relationship with Maryam, and I have to live with her a few more weeks."

For just a second, he looked at the floor and his mouth turned down. Then he was back to looking my way. "That sounds like a good idea."

And then I realized he wasn't looking at me but my desk. The spanking book sat there, right next to *Alice's Adventures in Wonderland*, which I was reading for Victorian Lit. He easily could read the spanking book's title on the spine. I decided not to say anything about it.

"I had a fun time with you today," I instead proffered.

"Me too. Look, would you like to do something together this evening? Just as friends? I'll order a pizza. I need to make it up to you for being a jerk."

"There's no need to make anything up to me, but if it means free pizza, I'm happy to let you assuage your guilt."

***

As I walked over to Clayton's dorm, everyone on campus seemed paired up and enjoying the warm spring day – couples held hands, kissed one another on the cheek, a guy's thumb hooked in his gal's back belt loop with palm resting across her jeaned derrière. A vision of Clayton spanking me flashed in my head. Would he be cheating on Maryam? If Maryam suspected Clayton of cheating on her, certainly she wouldn't guess it was me; I was far too bookish for a guy of his caliber.

Thinking about it is a waste of time. We've already agreed to keep everything platonic.

Once I arrived at this room, the aroma of fresh tomato sauce and cheese wafted through the doorway.

"Thanks for coming over," he said, as gently squeezing my shoulder. "Pizza just got here. Up for a movie?"

We browsed the Netflix offerings on his television while eating and ultimately settled on some British version of *Alice in Wonderland*. I kicked off my sandals and sat on his barrel chair that he probably got secondhand from his parents' house, while he took the floor in front of me.

"You'll have to tell me if the movie is anything like the book," he said.

My eyes widened, but I just played along. "Sure."

As the sky darkened outside, a cool air set in. Clayton closed the dorm window then when he saw I was crossing my arms to stay warm, got me a blanket from his bed. For a moment, I wished our friendship could be more.

With my legs tucked under me, eventually Clayton leaned back against the chair. Poor acting and special effects plagued the movie, and eventually I got bored. My leg shifted forward a little, and slowly I moved my foot toward his head and carefully grazed his ear with a toe.

His hand swiped back at my foot, and I let out a laugh. He turned to me, smiling. "I take it you're not enjoying the movie."

I shook my head.

"I'll find something else." With the remote, we started browsing again. My foot played a game of cat and mouse with his hand, as I tried to tickle his ear while he searched.

Eventually he grabbed my foot, and I yelped and laughed as trying to pull it away. Rather than let it go, though, his thumb pressed into my foot's underside, rubbing in circles up its length.

"Oooh," I let out, as my eyes closed, and I melted into his chair. "That feels so good."

"The book I wanted," he said, as continuing the

15

massage. "You have it, don't you?"

I blushed. "I've always wanted to know more about spanking. And sex."

His thumb reached my toes and rubbed one. "Has a man never made you cum, Allision?"

If he keeps this up, he very well might. "No," I somehow got out.

"Then let me be the first."

Clayton turned around, got on his knees. His fingers brushed my hair behind an ear, then he cupped the side of my cheek. Our lips met in a kiss, his lips warm and supple, and a shiver ran down my back.

Breaking our kiss, he leaned his forehead against mine, panting. "You have no idea how much I've wanted to do that."

"I think I do."

He kissed me again, lightly this time, just barely a touch of lips, growing more insistent with each second until our tongues entwined. His hands slipped under the blanket and unsnapped my jeans button. Pulling away from my mouth, he tugged my pants down my legs.

"Should we be doing this?" I said.

"Curiosity doesn't always kill the cat."

His fingers hooked into the side of my panties, and he took them down my legs as well. Then his hands slowly pushed my thighs apart, revealing my wet slit, and before I could think of anything to say, his mouth was upon it.

I no longer wanted to say anything.

Clayton's tongue slid up and down my slit, swiping

both sides of my vulva, and my mouth opened wide, letting go a long *Ahhh.* His tongue pressed in, circled the inside of my vagina, then swiped up until finding my clit, which he flicked.

"Oh fuck, that feels so good," I said, then his whole warm mouth was on my pussy again. My neck arched back, and his lips pressed in and again found my hard clit. He squeezed it between his lips. I let go a loud moan, then his tongue was back to flicking it.

With each swipe of his wet tongue across it, I gasped, didn't even realize he'd inserted two fingers into my hole. He curled his fingertips half back toward his palm and rubbed the top of my hole. My whole body tensed, as he found my G-spot.

He alternated swiping my clit and my G-spot, doing it just the way Maryam had described it being done to her. My breathing deepened, and I gripped the back his head, digging my nails into his black hair. Every muscle in my body spasmed and contracted, and a peaceful warmth engulfed me.

***

Clayton stood up, then after I caught my breath, I leaned into his torso. We wrapped our arms about one another.

"That was fantastic," I said, as he gently petted my hair. "How can I...*thank* you?" My hand caressed his hard cock.

Clayton's eyes closed as he moaned. "Maybe I'm not done...satisfying *you.*"

Mmm, that sounds good. "Earlier you said there were

some things Maryam wouldn't do. Maybe...I would."

He sat on the edge of his bed. "Come here."

I rose, and when I got to Clayton, his hand grabbed my wrist and the other my shoulder, then he pulled me down so my tummy was across his lap. I let out a yelp.

"Separate your legs," he said.

As I did so, my wet pussy gaped, fully exposed before him.

He pressed his palm into my shoulder blades, holding me in place as his other hand reached for something. I was able to turn my head just enough to see he'd grabbed a wooden spoon from beneath a pillow.

Hmmm, this should be interesting. No one has ever diddled my clit with a wooden spoon before.

Then *snap!* as the wooden spoon slapped against my ass, and I jerked upward on his lap. His hand was strong, though, and held me in place.

"This is for not being honest," he said.

Snap!

"Uh!" I winced then grit my teeth, as he struck my ass again.

My ass burned with pain, and the heat only rose, as he kept slapping it with the spoon. With each strike, I rose a little higher off his lap until his forearm pressed into my upper back, so that his weight held me down. My heart pounded, and a month went by in an instant.

Snap!

"This is for betraying your best friend," he said.

Snap!

My hand grabbed his legs, dug in.

"Why would you betray your best friend?" he asks.

Because I wanted to see if you were really like what she said, I wanted to say. But that would have been a lie, probably earning me a few more whacks.

So I lied.

"That's not the reason why," he said.

Snap!

"Is it?"

Snap!

My nipples hardened. "No," I whimpered.

Snap!

"Then what was it?"

"Because I wanted to know what it was like to be...spanked."

Snap!

"And what's it like?"

Snap!

His voice rose. "And what's it like?"

My ass sizzled from the hard smacks I'd so craved. "I'm excited...like I've never been before...like I've always *wanted* to be."

"Finally, you're telling the truth. Your juices are dripping down my thigh, you're so turned on. Have you had enough?"

Despite that my ass burned with pain, I suddenly felt...*comfortable.* Yes, that was the word for it. *Comfortable.* "I deserve...more."

Snap!

I breathed in through my clenched teeth as my haunches shook frantically.

He gave me four more whacks then lifted his forearm from my back. "Get on the bed, tummy down."

I wobbled onto the bed, holding my hand to my butt, feeling the heat rising from it. I laid down.

"Put your ass up in the air."

I shifted my knees closer to my waist, lifting my red butt. I heard his zipper being undone then his pants and belt buckle hitting the floor. He stepped out of his boxers and got on his knees behind me, ran the head of his cock against my slit.

"Your ass looks so damn hot all red like that." Clayton slowly slid in then almost all the way out. I moaned, bit my lower lip.

His cock pressed back in, and soon his thrusts fell into an urgent rhythm.

"Look back at me," he commanded. "Look back at me while I fuck you."

I looked over my shoulder at him, locking onto his gray eyes, groaning with each thrust. My eyes closed in pleasure.

"Keep them open," he said. "Keep looking at me."

I did, though with great difficulty.

"Ride my cock," he said and stopped thrusting.

My thighs and hips pushed me back on his cock then pistoned on it. His cock felt better than any fingers ever could. I picked up speed as he stood there, his head arched back, moaning.

An instant later, he pulled out and shot his hot load across my still burning ass cheeks.

Every one of my muscles tensed, as I shouted "Holy

fucking God" and spasmed. For several seconds, my body floated in a pool of warmth, then I collapsed to the mattress.

Catching his breath, Clayton stumbled over to his dresser and grabbed something. A moment later, he squirted lotion onto my ass cheeks, cooling the burn. His large hand stirred the lotion with his cum, mixing it, then rubbed the concoction into my skin.

***

In the quiet afterglow, he spooned me. I felt so safe…so complete…

"Thank you for letting me do that," he said.

"Thank you for doing that to me. It was…liberating."

I luxuriated a moment against his warm body and arms, as if they were a protective blanket.

"We just have one problem," I said.

He nodded. "Maryam."

"We can't tell her."

"Agreed."

"Good. And that itself creates a new problem."

He chuckled. "What's that?"

"We have to turn off our feelings – whether they're only sexual or not – for one another. I know that will be…difficult."

"I actually may have a solution for that."

"Oh?"

"Maryam always has wanted to try a three-way…with another woman."

I giggled. *Maybe there was hope for us after all.* "I can't wait to hear how you ask her about *that*."

Fisherman's Eyewash

You're driving me wild.

I want to shout it across the placid lake at Heath, his arm muscles bulging from broad shoulders, as he casts a fishing line into the water. But this is the trip we agreed to. This is what he enjoys doing, though I have no idea why. I'm a crowds-beneath-neon-lights-and-feet-atop-concrete kind of gal. So I stand on the stone step leading to the dock and content myself with watching him.

He sits still in the rowboat, as if meditating. Occasionally, there is a *plop* in the water – from what I don't know, maybe a diving insect or a fish hitting the surface – and it sends out a small ripple. The lake and our cabin is so quiet I swear I can hear the sun slowly rising. In other words, boring as hell.

Still, I smile. He looks happy, *natural*, out there, dressed in flannel shirt and straw stem stuck between his teeth.

***

That's not surprising, given how out of place he looked when I first met him at a cocktail party all those months ago…

He stands alone, off to the side, a gentle giant. He has the most piercing blue eyes I've ever seen, and I like the size of his hands. So I walk right up to him.

"I can see that you're handsome, but what else should I know about you?" I say.

He smirks, and I swear turns a shade red. "Aren't I the one who's supposed to deliver the pickup line?"

I almost shiver at his deep voice. "If you did, what line would you use?"

He gazes at me for a long moment. "Okay. Kiss me if I'm wrong, but fish can fly, right?"

I chuckle. "That's so cheesy, I actually like it."

He extends a hand. "I'm Heath."

I stare at his big mitt for a moment. Nobody shakes hands at cocktail parties. Still, I take it. My own looks tiny in his, like a lost girl's hand would in a policeman's. "Breanne," I say in a half-whisper.

***

For the first time in several minutes, he moves, winding the handle on his reel. I'm not sure why he would need to do that. I've never asked. In fairness, he's never asked me about why I need to do certain things. He just accepts it.

A light mist rises off the lake, and I think back to our first night together, when fog keeps us from venturing out.

His hand caresses the back of my neck, and the tips of his fingers play gently with my hair. I breathe out and close my eyes. His face slowly closes on mine, but before our lips meet, I kiss him with a wide open mouth and adventurous tongue.

My jeans are skin tight, allowing me to feel the shape

of his equipment, as I grind against him. He swells, and I reach down to feel him. We stand there, the world spinning around us, tasting each other. My hand slips inside his pants.

As I stroke his dick, he groans then closes his hand around my breast and squeezes, oh so delicately.

Rather than pout, my free hand slides to the back of his head and pushes him deeper inside my mouth, as I stroke him inside his jeans with two fingers.

He pulls back and swats my butt.

My eyes fly open, and there he is, still in the rowboat, having not moved at all.

I sit on the stone step, it hard against my ass with only my thin nightie providing a cushion. After a moment, I cradle my chin in a hand. Acceptance is approval, if only tacit, right?

***

No matter how hard I try, I can't make him mad.

"You're selling yourself short," I say after we've moved in together, arms folded.

"I don't want to sit penned in some corporate office working numbers all day. C'mon, you know me – that's not who I am."

I do know him. *That's why I have to do this.* "You could make six figures a year, easily."

"Money isn't what happiness is about."

"Neither is poverty."

"We already make plenty to meet our needs."

Perfect, he's exposed himself for the dagger. "You mean *I* make plenty to meet our needs." That always worked on my ex.

He pauses for a moment. "Do you think it's unfair that you're contributing more than I am?"

Dagger deflected. He knew I actually liked being the breadwinner. "No...I uh, look, you're smart and have the presence of authority to do it, that's all." Truth is, he makes plenty as a first-line manager.

The problem is that he lacks the – no strike that – he *possesses* the principles that prevent him from taking such a higher-level position.

For a moment, a look of confusion covers his face then he suddenly looks like a kicked puppy. "Are you saying you're...unhappy with me? With..."

He doesn't finish his sentence, but I do in my head... *who I am. ...Are you saying you're unhappy with who I am?*

My whole being suddenly feels hollow. "Oh God no, that's not it at all." I wrap my arms about his waist as falling into him. "That's not it at all, baby."

He holds me and pats my back, though I know he is still confused. I can feel it in the way his arms hang there, loose and tentative.

***

As the sun lights up more of the lake and surrounding pine forest, birdsong fills the air, sporadic at first but slowly expanding in number and volume across the trees. Heath still hasn't moved. His patience astounds me, always has.

Then a large white bird with brown wings – an osprey I think Heath called it – plunges into the lake, shattering its flatness, and rises out, a fish in its talons. Waves from the dive splash against the shore, as the bird disappears around a curve in the bay.

The waves take me back to when Heath and I walked on the beach together, hand in hand at sunset. He likes being by water. I don't know why. *I don't care why, just so long as this moment never ends.*

And then it does.

"You never tell me much about yourself," he says.

My mind stutter steps, and I gulp. "What do you want to...know?"

He shrugs. "Anything. Everything. It's not so much what I want to know than it is why you don't say much about yourself."

I fake a giggle, hope he doesn't pick up on it. "There's not much to say really."

I give him a big smile, gaze at him, hoping he won't ask anymore. His stubbled jawline and sun-kissed skin stirs something inside me.

Before he can respond, I fall forward. His quick reflexes catch me, his strong arms hold me up.

"Are you all right?" he asks.

I look back. "A piece of driftwood was half-buried in the sand. I didn't see it."

We keep walking, quietly.

Then he says, "Why were you trying to make me mad at you the other night?"

My face blushes. *Because maybe then you'd give me what I desired, what I needed.* "I'm sorry, I shouldn't have done that."

"Apology accepted. But you haven't answered my question."

I need a diversion. "I appreciate how you didn't get mad at me actually."

His nose and forehead scrunch up. "So it was a test?"

I run with it. "Uh-huh."

"To see if I'd lose my temper?"

"You didn't have any 'temper' at all."

"And that's a bad thing?"

Is it? Sometimes I just want to scream, to throw every breakable object I can grab, to tell the world, "It's unfair! It's unfair that you make me keep this secret!"

"No," I say. "It's a good thing."

***

Sometimes when holding a secret from others, you come to believe that it's really someone else's. You don't believe who you actually are.

Then you don't know who you are at all.

Heath pays no attention to the diving wild bird. Then his line shifts, like something is yanking it underwater, and his big hands go into action, winding the reel. Something splashes out of the water; it must be a fish, and he recoils as water flies at him.

I wonder if he recoiled that time he got hull cleaner in his eye. I am on the sofa, reading a book, when he races into the house, the door slamming behind him. A fist covers his eye.

I quickly follow him into the bathroom where he clumsily cups water in his palm and tosses it into his eye. "What happened?"

"Cleaning gel got in my eye while washing the rowboat," he manages, as bringing another palmful of water to his face.

I throw open the medicine cabinet door and grab a bottle of eyewash. "Hold your head back, keep your eye open."

He does, and I squirt the saline solution straight at his pupil.

"Ow! That burns! I ought to take you over me knee!"

"Promises, promises," I joke, but he's in no mood for humor.

He brings a towel to his eye. "Sorry," he says. "I didn't mean to snap at you."

Well, I almost got him mad.

"And thanks. The solution actually did the trick."

I shrug. "It's one of my little secrets."

***

Health's fishing line is taut as it zigs one way then the next while he reels. Then the line goes limp, and sunlight flashes off the empty hook. The one that got away.

I can't let him get away. Which means I can't tell him.

Heath slowly ran his fingers along my ear lobe as my head rests on his chest, both of us slowly catching our breath and coming down from the high of our mutual orgasm. My hand plays with his pubic hair as I listen to his heartbeat slow. The sun through the windows warms us and the rumpled sheets.

"Can I ask you a question, Heath?"

His fingers momentarily stop. "Sure baby."

"Why do you love me?"

He says nothing for a long moment, like he's deep in thought. "Because you complete me."

I stare at the piece of driftwood hanging on the far wall. Heath brought it back from his Northwoods cabin, hung it there not so much as decoration but as a reminder of what he loves, of who he is.

He doesn't ask me why I love him. He doesn't ask why I posed the question.

He places bait on the hook and recasts the line.

**

Several minutes later, Heath's line goes taut again, and the whirring of the reel as a fish tries to pull away fills the air. His hands work the handle, though, and after the struggling fish slaps the surface a couple of times, it's suddenly in the air at the rod's tip. Heath brings the rod over the rowboat, unhooks the fish, and tosses it into a pail. After setting the rod aside, his hands take the oars...

...just like they took my waist, as he nuzzles my neck from behind, his warm, tender lips trailing along my exposed skin, then he whispers in my ear, "I'm going to run my hands all over your body, Breanne, especially where you like to be touched, and then use my fingers to tease you until you're ready for more. Then I'll put my fingers inside you and fuck you with them until you orgasm."

My eyes close as I melt into him. "Is that all you're going to do to me?"

After sex, he gently strokes my hair, as we spoon. His

semi-hard cock rests against my ass.

Emboldened by our intimacy, I tell him what I like…what I want. He just nods.

And listens.

There is no frat boy "That's hot!" There is no cringe followed by an anxious-ridden question if I've been abused.

Because I haven't been. I just enjoy it. That's who I am.

***

Heath wraps the mooring line around a pole on the dock, ties it off. I wait for him to step off with pail in hand and then stand. I wiggle the nightie off my shoulders, and it slips to the stone step, puddling at my feet.

He stops, taking in my naked figure, then sets down the pail and a moment later is kissing the nape of my neck. I place my hands on his hips and pull him close, intent and focused, and we tilt our heads and close our eyes, as I press my lips against his. The contact is short and meaningful, with a gentle touch of tongues as I drag my hand down his cheek. We pull away, studying each other in the aftermath, my lips registering the sensation and storing his taste.

Salt and earth. His kiss tastes like salt and earth.

***

It's a secret you must always carry.

You can't tell family. They'll wonder if something happened to you, who the culprit might be, then one will take your hand and quietly suggest therapy.

You can't tell your best girlfriend because she'll look aghast at you, for no self-respecting woman – certainly not one with a college education and who's in middle management – should ever want that.

You can't tell a man you date because he'll think you're kinky and will do anything with him. And then he'll force you to.

So you go about your day hiding who you are, letting people only see a mask that you wear to protect you, to project an image of who they want to see.

There are no annual parades declaring pride in who you are, no one on afternoon talk shows normalizing this, no bestselling books that tout you as a heroic main character, no academic studies acknowledging it so you can settle in some nice, liberal college town and not have to worry about others staring judgmentally at you when you walk down the street.

There's just you.

Just you alone.

***

My back is on the stone step above him, and his large hands have separated my legs so he can kiss my inner thighs. My dampness grows.

His tongue easily slips between my pussy lips and finds my urethra. He lightly drags his tongue's tip up one side then above it and down the other side. I moan as my eyes close.

Then his tongue repeats the maneuver in reverse, barely grazing my U-spot as he returns to his start point. He does it one more time then once more. My breathing grows ragged.

He softly and slowly tongues me from left to right then right to left, as if he were licking an ice-cream cone. Then, at top of my U-spot, his tongue gently goes up and hits my clit.

My back arches and muscles tense, and as he pulls away, I ejaculate, shoot straight out into his eye as he stares down my vagina.

He jumps back, and the back of his hand flies to that eye to rub it out.

I sit up. "Oh my God, Heath, I'm sorry, I didn't mean to; it just felt so good."

He stands, shakes his head, blinks rapidly.

I rise, my hands trembling. "Do you need eyewash?"

Heath grins, lets out a chuckle. "No, I think I got that already."

I'm not sure if I should laugh or not, if –

Before I can finish my thought, he wraps his hand around the back of my neck, guides me to a tree, and leans me over a thick, low-lying branch. I watch him from the corner of my eye as he steps away. Is he going to use his fishing rod?

Instead, he stops at a shrub, snaps off a small branch. His hand quickly strips away the leaves, then from his pocket he pulls fishing line and binds the bare side branches tightly together. He inspects his handiwork then whaps it in a palm.

Ah, the sweet sound it makes.

I imagine that sound as the branches swing through the air and the pain it will cause on my bare behind. My pussy drips.

Heath swings the birch forward, it whirring, but his wrist pulls up at the last second, and all I feel on my tush is the air of it passing. He swings again, and I gasp prematurely, expecting the pain, but again he pulls up at the last moment, though the birch rod grazes my behind. He holds the rod there for a moment.

His third swing hits my ass hard. "Uhn!" I wince, as a hot line burns across my tush.

The next swing comes quickly, before I catch my breath. And then another swing. The pain ripples through my ass and body. My hear pounds faster, and my moans grow louder.

He pauses a moment, lets me linger in the burn. Before it fully dissipates, he winds up and strikes again, lower on my ass. I jerk as yelping.

My ass is red for sure. My pussy grows wetter still.

Heath taps the birch rod over the spots he's hit, and I flinch, for the skin is tender.

Then the spanking begins anew. His strikes go up and down my ass and on to my upper thigh. My toes at first dig into the soil but then my feet dance. As my squeals grow loud, echoing along the trees, he stops, allowing my breathing to calm.

The songbirds continue their symphony, oblivious to us.

He swings the birch rod, and I flinch in anticipation, but he stops before making contact. I'm breathing quickly, and my breasts, fuller now, weigh heavy from my chest.

Then he quick swings again, and I yelp. He runs the rod up and down my ass and thigh, swings, pulls up, and I flinch again in anticipation.

He's breaking me.

He delivers a series of short but harsh strikes, first at the center of an ass cheek, then just below the back then on the underside of the other cheek, then on the opposite thigh. I recoil with each stroke, and the pain is overwhelming as I try catching my breath in a sob. My muscles tense.

"What are you?" he asks nonchalantly.

I say nothing, hold back the tears.

He taps my ass lightly. "What are you?"

I won't say.

He strikes hard, and I jerk forward then stiffen, as pleasure ripples through my body. My orgasm is like a shattering. A long moan fills the air, slowly expanding in volume across the trees and over the lake, my sobs turning into a hard cry that won't stop.

Heath tosses the birch into the bushes then grabs my hair and pulls me up off the branch. He draws me into him, kisses my cheeks, and with the back of his thumb gently wipes the tears from my face.

"I'm a spanko," I say.

He wraps his arms under my knees and lifts me into his arms. My hands arc around his neck, as my head cradles against his shoulder.

"Let's go put some salve on that," he says.

"Okay," I whimper.

I am free.

Come Hither

Beneath the banner that says *Congratulations Liliana*, Manuel – a decade older since my crush on him began – converses with a neighbor. Silver already shows on Manuel's temples, not surprising after what he's been through, but he retains his radiant brown eyes. I look away, don't want to get caught staring, though that is difficult given the hard body his tailored clothing accentuates. Manuel moves on to speak with someone else, probably an old acquaintance, as I don't recognize her. In fact, I don't recognize almost anyone here and wonder a moment if people came less for Liliana's graduation than to check in on her father.

And the woman he's talking with seems to be checking him out a bit much. Did she just touch his arm and laugh a little too loud?

I don't care. Liliana's father always was a no-fly zone. That woman didn't just flip her hair back, did she? Well, maybe I care a little.

Manuel moves on to the next person, just one step away from me. Okay, time to think of something to say. *When I was sucking my boyfriend's cock in college this year, I imagined it was yours.* No, that won't do.

And then he's standing before me, his smile delectable. "Caitlyn! How are you?" His hug is tentative.

"You must have graduated this spring too?"

"No, I'm on the five-year plan. I'm not quite as motivated as Liliana."

His expression turns serious. "She really dived into her studies after Mrs. Lopez passed..." He does a sign of the cross, and his eyes look like tears will fall from them. "...bless her soul. I think it was a way for Liliana to keep her mind off her mother."

I imagine myself on all fours as he fucks me from behind, his large hand slapping my ass.

Back to reality, Caitlynn. I nodded. "We've talked a little about her mother." *And a little about how you're lonely.*

"You've always been there for Liliana. She is lucky to have such a good friend."

Guilt trickles through me. Not that good of a friend when I think about her father the way I do. But I just smile.

A woman steps almost between us, her back to my face. "Manuel! It's so good to see you again. I so hope everything is going well. You won't believe what my committee has planned for the fundrais–"

She's almost twice my age, and that alone gives her a better shot with Liliana's father than I'll ever have. Speaking of Liliana, where is she? I turn away to look for her, but as my gaze sweeps over the room then behind Manuel, he stretches his neck around her, starts to say something. The woman steps in front of him, so I can't read his lips. Fortune favors the bold, I guess, or at least the brash.

"Caitlynn!" Liliana exclaims from halfway across the room and waves me over.

I make my way through the crowd. When we're a foot away from one another, we scream each other's name and embrace in a bear hug.

"Congratulations on graduating, Liliana," I say as we separate. "Who are all of these people?"

"Dad's friends," she says. "A few family and neighbors. So this is it – the last weekend."

"The last weekend?"

"My last weekend in town. I'm leaving Monday morning for Chicago to find an apartment."

"Leaving already?"

"I start Tuesday, remember?"

"*This* Tuesday?"

She nods.

"I thought we'd have more time together, until the end of May at least."

"I want to get started right away."

Of course you do. You don't want to stay here where there are so many memories. "Tuesday, huh? Well, that gives you a little time to recover from this weekend's hangover."

"Oh don't look so sad. I'm sure you're going to spend the summer with that hot Louis."

"*Luis*. Luis and I broke up a month ago."

"A month ago? How did I miss that?"

"I didn't make a big deal out of it. He was...all right."

Liliana touches my forearm. "Don't be down – that you broke up is a good thing actually. Now we can hang out together in Chicago as two bachelorettes, do the *Sex in the City* thing."

Actually, this city is just fine for sex. I glance at Manuel, who another woman has honed in on.

***

I slide onto my bed, head spinning from all of the drinks at Liliana's party. For a moment, I try to focus on a poster of some boy band that had lost its flavor sometime during my freshman year of college. I'm surprised I hadn't changed them over the years but then even at this moment I don't want to. Maybe I'm still clinging to something.

Focusing just increases the spinning, so I close my eyes. That helps. My mind drifts to nothingness, and then his hand touches my cheek, traces his broad palm down to the line of my neck. It's an old fantasy, one I've had many times in this bedroom. I shudder as his other hand skims down my shoulder and skims the top of a breast with his fingertips.

My breathing deepens. I try not to relive it, but maybe it's the alcohol. His mouth covers a nipple, hands kneading the breast beneath it, and I arch into his touch.

He whispers in my ear, "Get on all fours."

I turn over, get on my knees and elbows, as his large hand caresses my thigh then comes up to my mound. A finger dips inside, finds my clit.

I gasp.

He circles it, slowly at first. My heart thuds faster.

Thwack!

His other hand slaps my ass. "You're a bad girl,

Caitlynn, wanting this."

A second finger enters me, and bending at the knuckle, the pair in a come hither motion rubs my clit up and down. I gasp.

Thwack!

"Tell me what you are, Caitlynn."

I can barely get it out between my moans. "I'm – I'm a – bad girl."

Thwack!

"And why are you a bad girl, Caitlynn?"

"Be – because – I – want this."

Thwack!

I stiffen, then a wave of pleasure overtakes me. My body seems to float softly to the bed, as my panting slows. After a moment, I remove my wet fingers from between my legs and roll over.

His brown eyes stare down as me.

"Thank you," I say, "thank you Manuel."

***

The sun shines bright early Wednesday morning, as I walk our aussiedoodle Carly past Liliana's house. I think of the playdates, the birthday parties, the sleepovers Liliana and I shared there over the years. I frown at the thought of her mother, who jogged every morning when I walked Carly back then, and how cancer had reduced her to a wisp of who she was. Manuel must have felt so helpless, had been so lonely, during that time.

"Caitlynn!" he shouts to me through a window. "Wait up!"

A few seconds later, he exits the front door. My eyes

stick to the muscled contours shown by his rolled-up sleeves. He's always looked damn good in a button-up shirt.

"Caitlynn," he says, his voice like velvet, "I just want to apologize."

And I want to run my fingers through your hair, to hold your head between my legs until I am satisfied.

But then I'm back to reality. He wants to apologize? "For what?" I say. Why didn't I shower before walking Carly? Damn, I must smell. Hopefully he thinks it's Carly.

"We were talking, and Leann Cunningham interrupted. I didn't have the chance to say goodbye. Worse, I didn't feel like we had finished our conversation."

There wasn't much else to say, except maybe *Do you like doggy style?*

"There's no need to apologize; I wasn't offended." Definitely not offended. Maybe confused with a pinch of nervousness and a heavy dash of arousal, but not offended. "I understand."

"No, there really was no excuse. For the last four years, Leann has been trying to get me to go out with her. I don't know why I put up with her anymore."

Relief washes through me. Good, he's not attracted to her. "But don't you get lonely?"

I can't believe I just said that.

His face flushes. "Yes, of course. And I'm ready to move on. But she's not the one."

"Is there...someone?"

I can't believe I just said that too. Shut up, Caitlynn!

Manuel shakes his head. "No. I need someone I can talk to yet someone who also can make me feel young again. Leann Cunningham is about country club parties, and she's the one who does all of the talking." He smells like cinnamon, and I want to bite him.

"Oh," is all I manage to get out.

Manuel kneels to Carly, his large hands rubbing her jowls. I imagine those large hands trailing up my waist then kneading my breasts. He's got Carly's tail a waggin'. And now he knows she's not the one who smells.

He rises. "Thank you for stopping and accepting my apology." His hand touches my bare arm.

Go on, grab my arm, turn me around and slap my behind.

Manuel returns to his house, and after a moment I continue walking Carly, all cold and empty inside. What an idiot I am, thinking what I did about my best friend's dad as he tried to apologize, as he tried to be a gentleman. To think that anything ever could happen between us is foolish, I tell myself yet again. I no longer feel like the smart, educated college student I am but a dorky teenage girl.

***

On my knees in Luis's dorm room, I stroke his cock with my hand, lick the entire shaft, tease the head with my tongue, then put the entire thing in my mouth as far as I can and slowly draw back from it. As he moans, I repeat those motions.

I feel his cockhead grow in size, as it slips off my tongue. "Are you close baby?" I say.

His eyes are closed and head arched back. "Huh-huh," he barely gets out.

"I want you to cum in my mouth, Manuel," I say and slowly take it back into me.

His hips stop gyrating, and I look up at him, his cock half in my mouth. "What did you say?"

I let his member fall from my lips. "I said I want you to cum in my mouth." I lift his cock to my lips.

He steps back. "No, after that."

I gaze at him quizzically.

"You called me 'Manuel.'"

"I did?"

He nods. "Who the hell is Manuel?"

Perfect. Now he'll be mad at me. I giggle. "Just a slip of the tongue." I giggle again at the double entendre and lay my torso over his mattress so my ass is sticking out. "Guess you'll have to punish me with a spanking for that."

I wiggle my butt.

He slaps my ass. Not very hard, but enough to get my juices going. There's another slap. I feel...subversive.

I wiggle my butt again. "Are you just going to tickle me or am I going to get a spanking?"

Whack!

His large palm hits my ass full on, and I wince at the sting. And then, as if I've just drank a glass of cold water on the hottest day of summer, my body suddenly feels so good.

Whack!

I moan as the burn gives way to the warmth of

pleasure. I want to say *Thank you, Manuel* but know better than to push my luck.

Whack!

And then my hands fly to the back of my head, the fingers interlocking as Luis keeps striking me. I don't know why I do it; it's an involuntary response, like a knee jerking to a doctor's reflex hammer.

And then, when there should be another *whack,* there is nothing.

"What are you doing?" Luis said.

"Huh?" I look over my shoulder, rub my red ass.

"You were holding your hands behind your head."

"Yeah, so?"

"It was...weird, that's all."

I turn to fully face him. His cock has gone soft.

***

I check the time on my smartphone yet again as the country club crowd mingled at the fundraiser Leann Cunningham had planned. How my parents talked me into going with them escapes me at the moment. The fundraiser decor is well themed, I admit, as I gaze at the black and gold balloons and crepe paper bunting lining the head table. Loud laughs increasingly fill the banquet hall, as the booze flows. Give that Leann credit – people are more likely to part with their money when a little buzzed, so schedule the auction well after the open bar begins serving.

I head out onto the verandah for some quiet so I can scroll my phone. It's crowded near the doors where the umbrella-covered tables and seats are, so I go to the far end that wraps around the country club's side.

As I turn the corner, I stop. Manuel leans on the railing, a bottle of beer in one hand, staring into the horizon. He appears to be contemplating something.

Don't bother him during such a personal moment, I tell myself. But then what had Liliana once told me – that he was lonely all the time? Well, that makes two of us.

"Mr. Lopez?"

He looks up and smiling, waves me over. "Caitlynn, good to see you. Are you as bored as I am?"

"Guess Miss Cunningham did not have the two of us in mind when she set this up."

He chuckles. I watch his chest ripple beneath his dress shirt, of which he's undone the top couple of buttons. I catch a whiff of his cinnamon scent in the light breeze.

"Liliana just left Monday, and I already miss her," he says then takes a long swig of his beer. "Her leaving is like losing Mrs. Lopez all over again."

My hear melts in sadness. "I...I miss Liliana too" then quickly add, "and Mrs. Lopez."

He nods. "Liliana tells me I should start dating again." He almost sounds angry.

My mouth parts in surprise. She said that?

"And she's right, I should. It's only out of guilt that I've been faithful to her mother's memory."

"That's quite romantic," I say, almost swooning. *Come on, Mr. Lopez, bend me over the railing and take me right now.*

Oh God, did I just say or think that?

He doesn't seem to notice. "And the funny thing is Mrs. Lopez would have said the same thing."

"She would?"

He slowly nods. "She and Liliana always thought alike. And their attitude always was 'Get over it, move on.'"

I swallow hard. "Are you ready? To...move on?"

He says nothing for a long moment. "I'm not sure. Sometimes I think I am; sometimes I wish for the way things were."

The sunlight burns warm on my cheek. Wishing for the way things were might also mean wishing for how things will be. I need to lighten the mood. "Maybe you just need someone to nudge you along," I say, half giggling.

He looks at me. "You mean someone like Leann Cunningham?"

My stomach feels like it's dropped four stories in an instant. "Um, probably not her."

Manuel laughs, fully and from the belly, and I join him. His hand touches my bare arm, and lightning strikes my body. "No, probably not her," he says, and his hand returns to his side.

A coldness rushes over me.

He needs to heal, I realize. *I can help him heal.*

"Caitlynn!" my mother says from several feet behind me.

I turn.

"Oh hi Manuel," she says. "They're going to start the

auction in a few moments. The two of you come join us."

Us. Meaning her and my father. Two people who should be and are together joined by two people who shouldn't be and aren't. Oh, the universe is cruel.

***

I'm naked in my dorm room, both my hands gripping the dresser top as my butt sticks out. Luis slaps it, but the sting feels more like poke than a whack. I remain patient, as he thumps each cheek at a lackadaisical pace. There's no adrenaline surge from it, and the only heightened emotion and sensation I feel is frustration.

What the fuck is wrong with him?

"Harder," I say.

He complies, and that sear of pain spikes then drifts into the warmth of pleasure. There can be a fine line between pleasure and pain, and the difference between a good and a bad spanking is which side of the line it falls on.

Luis whacks me again, and I flinch then relish the burn and what it means. I wonder if anyone passing the room in the dorm hallway heard that sweet smack of hard palm against my soft bum. The V between my legs grows wet.

And then he's back to those baby slaps, those stupid, worthless wimpy slaps. I spin toward him. "What's wrong?"

He steps back, gestures toward me with a grimace. "*This* is wrong."

"Spanking? You're not turned on by it?"

"Not exactly," he hisses.

I glance at his cock. He *isn't* turned on. "I thought you'd like it. You get to be in control."

"Except I'm not, am I?" His jaw clenches.

"What do you mean?"

"It's you who enjoys it. It's you who gets all turned on by it."

"And what's wrong with that?"

"I'm not enjoying it."

"And you think I enjoy being on my knees sucking your cock?"

"You don't?"

Oh Jesus Christ. "No." OK, I do a little. But maybe if I get him mad again he'll turn me around and give me the spanking I crave.

The vein on his neck bulges, and he pulls on his boxers.

"What are you doing? You're not leaving?"

He tugging his jeans up his legs should have told me the answer is *yes.*

"Oh don't be this way. Stay."

Luis surprises me with the speed his sandals and white tee go on. He heads to the door, and I'm sure as he opened it that some guy passing by got a good look at me naked.

Maybe he'd be willing to spank me?

***

Trying to stay cool during the unseasonably sultry weather, I wear a sundress and flip-flops as walking Carly. All weekend I thought about Manuel and wonder if I'll see him as Liliana's house comes in sight. I ponder if she'll text me like she promised at the party.

And then I stop, listen closely. Is that crying coming from the upstairs window? Carly cocks her ear too.

I head to the front door, turn the knob, and walk in, just like I always did whenever Liliana invited me over. There was no need to lock a door in our neighborhood. Inside, I let Carly off her leash, and she goes about sniffing the floor, disappearing into the living room.

The sobbing grows louder, as I quietly walk upstairs. At the top, I turn toward Manuel's office, and there is his, sitting in his plush lather chair, head in hands.

I stand in the doorway. "Manuel? Are you all right?"

He looks up, his face red from too many tears. "Caitlynn?"

"I was walking Carly and thought I heard someone crying. Are you all right?"

He pulls a tissue from a box on his desk, wipes his eyes. "Yes, everything is okay."

"No it's not. Why are you crying?"

"I...no, it's silly. It's nothing. Thank you for checking on me, though." He chuckles. "I'm getting old and suppose that'll be the case more and more now."

"You're not old." I enter his office, stand next to him. His cinnamon scent swirls in my nostrils, making me heady. "What's wrong? I won't tell anyone else."

His watery brown eyes gaze at him. "I was just thinking that...that I will be lonely the rest of my life."

My heart turns to putty. "You don't have to be alone."

"I know, I know...I just can't bring myself to...try."

"You just need someone to help you through that."

He gazes off into space, as if contemplating it. "I couldn't do that to someone, to *use* them."

"Even if they *wanted* to be used?"

He looks at me again, an eyebrow raised. His Fighting Illini T-shirt does nothing to hide his muscled physique. *Fortune favors the bold*, I tell myself.

With that, I pull the sundress over my head and stand in front of him naked but for my bra and lace panties.

***

Manuel's eyes widen. "Caitlynn, I–"

"Shh," I say and lean forward, giving him a glimpse at my cleavage, and softly kiss him on the lips. My hand delicately caresses his cheek.

His firm hand rises to my bare waist, and I kiss him again. This time, his lips willingly participate.

I take his free hand into mine. "For years I've had a crush on you, Manuel. Let me...*help you* through this." I slowly pull his arm as stepping back.

He rises from the plush leather chair. His half-hard member bulges in his shorts. "Caitlynn, there's–"

I bring a finger to his mouth. Biting my lip, my finger traces down the side of his neck. I grin at his shiver. "Shh. Let me show you how much...I've wanted you."

He strokes my hair. "Caitlynn, you've grown into a beautiful young woman. But–"

I am losing him. Desperation keeps me from thinking straight, and so I go with the first thing that comes to mind. I undo my bra, let it tumble to the carpet, then reach my hand around to the back of his head, push it to my breasts.

His warm breath washes over my bare skin, and my eyes close.

A moment later, his large hands wrap around my waist and his lips press against my nipple. I gasp, head arcing to the ceiling, reveling in the feel of his lips pulling on me.

"Yes, kiss my nipples," I say.

Then, without warning, he sucks hard, and I cry out, almost buckling. He moves to the other breast, and I gaze at the crown of his head, refusing to let him go. His teeth pinch my nipple, just hard enough that pain and pleasure mix. My head rolls back again, as I moan. His mouth takes in more of my breast, and he alternately sucks and pulls as his other hand firmly grips my waist.

"Talk dirty to me," I say in just above a whisper.

His lips pinch my breasts with his nipple fully in his mouth, as his tongue flicks it to a hardened point. Eyes closed, I whimper.

He pulls back, my quivering hand too weak to hold it in place. "Oh yeah, you like it like that, don't you?"

I only answer with a caress of his hair, it so soft and thick.

His lips kiss their way down my toned tummy to the top of my panties. He drops to his knees, hooks his thumbs into the panties' sides, and slowly pulls them down – well, more like slides them down given how wet I am – until gravity does the rest.

"Is this what you've fantasized about?" he says.

"No," I mewl, as he kisses my thighs, "it's better."

His mouth reaches my mound, lathes it with kisses.

My knees quiver, and I hold onto his head to keep from falling.

Manuel makes the Boy Scout sign with two fingers and with palm up slowly presses then into my slit. My vagina muscles clench them as my fingernails dig into his head. His fingers, fully in me, sit still for a moment, then as withdrawing he curls them up, as if beckoning someone to come hither, rubbing my G-spot.

I gasp in pleasure, nearly fall over.

His tongue finds my clit, licks it in slow circles, as he again inserts his fingers then curls and pulls them back, rubbing my G-spot once more.

My moan is so loud, I'm sure someone outside could hear it.

"Do you like that?"

"Yes," I'm able to get out between ragged breaths.

He keeps working his tongue on my clit as softly petting my G-spot, and soon I find myself floating, as if on a gentle wave in the ocean. With each wave, my muscles grew tenser, and then suddenly my hands and feet spasm, and all of the tension releases, as a I let go a loud scream.

I mold my body into his, as my heart slows.

His warm lips kiss my tummy. "Tell me what you fantasize about."

My face reddens, but I'm too far gone to care. "You...call me a naughty girl. You...spank me."

***

I come up from Luis' crotch, his cum dripping from my lips, his softening cock in my hand, and smile.

"You liked that, didn't you?" he says.

I shrug. "I liked pleasing you."

He chuckles.

I got up and place my hands on the wall then lean forward so the butt juts out. "My turn?"

"'My turn' what?"

"You know." I look over my shoulder at him and wiggle my butt.

Luis rolls his eyes. "Not again."

"What? I pleased you, now it's your turn to please me."

"I *already* did."

Standing straight, I turn to him. "How so?"

"You gave me a blow job."

"And how is that pleasing *me*?"

"You said you enjoyed it."

"I said I enjoyed pleasing you. That's because I love you." I set my hands back on the wall. "Now get off your ass and start pleasing me because *you* love me."

"I don't enjoy doing that."

"And you think I enjoyed you cumming in my mouth?"

"You did enjoy it."

"No, I *didn't*."

Luis got up and started dressing. Oh, not this again.

"What the fuck, Luis? You're going to cum in my mouth and then walk out on me?"

And then it dawns on me. Luis is one of those men who believes a woman's pleasure comes from her pleasing him – *not* he pleasing her.

He already is pulling up his jeans when I turn back to him. Luis is a fast dresser, especially during a confrontation.

I wipe his cum off my chin with the back of my hand. "If you walk out that door, Luis, we're through. It's over between us."

He just grunts, as he ties his tennis shoes then buttons up his shirt. A moment later, he slams the door behind him.

We never speak again.

***

Manuel wraps his muscled arm around my legs, lifts me as he stands. Carrying me over his shoulders, he takes me to the office's sofa, and a sandal slips off my foot. In one swift motion, he sits and swings me tummy down over his knees, and the other sandal flies across the room.

For a moment, Manuel stares at my perky ass, then caresses its milky smoothness. He slaps a butt cheek a couple of times, not too hard, but enough to get my attention, and I let go a quick squeal at each one.

His palm continues to gently massage my ass, as if he were afraid he'd hurt me. Oh God, don't turn into Luis on me.

"You're such a naughty girl," he says.

Then he slaps the other cheek twice, and my gasps turn to short moans. I feel his dick hardening against my tummy.

Manuel caresses my ass again then a finger dips into my pussy and rubs against the clit. My ass involuntarily rises to meet him, as I groan deeply.

Then his fingers leave my wetness and slap my cheeks again in quick succession. I yelp as my nails dig deep into the sofa cushion.

He squeezes my ass cheeks then separates them, exposing my brown spot and my soaked slit. His finger slips into my pussy again and rubs my clit over and over, and I bury my face into his muscled leg as moaning.

But no sooner than I start gyrating against the finger then he pulls out and slaps my butt cheeks again, sending waves of pain through me. He squeezes my burning flesh, separates my cheeks once more, then slaps them again, this time harder. I yelp loudly.

No, he's no Luis. He is a *man*.

His finger circles my clit again, and my hips thrust, trying to find something to fill the wet emptiness between my legs, and I gasp in pleasure. Then he slaps my ass, canceling with a new pain any pleasure I felt.

My hands fly to the back of my head, the fingers interlocking, as he keeps striking me. And then the pain fades into pleasure as his finger rubs against my clit. I buck again as moaning.

His free hand presses against my lower back, holding me in place, but it's not enough to keep me from moving. Then his free hand slaps my butt as his other hand rubs my clit

My body turns into a soppy mess as both pain and pleasure ripple through me while he masturbates and spanks me at the same time.

Yes, the pain is my punishment, my punishment for seducing him, for keeping him from being faithful to his wife's memory. And the pleasure is my reward for helping him heal.

"You are a naughty girl. You like being a naughty girl, don't you?"

A swell of heat pulses through my body, as I moan.

"Do you want me to make you cum?"

"Yes," I somehow get out between breaths, as his finger flicks my clit back and forth over and over.

Every muscle in my body – including some I didn't even know until that moment existed –

tenses. An instant later, the explosion hits. I scream.

He just lets me lay there, caresses my back and sore ass, as I catch my breath and the dizziness subsides. Then, he helps me turn over so I'm sitting on his lap, and once I wrap my arms around his neck, he does the same with his arms about my back and legs then stands.

A few steps later, he sets me down at the edge of his bed. Unbuckling his jeans, they drop to the floor, and then he tugs his boxers down, revealing his magnificent, veined cock, it fully engorged, his testicles hanging low below them.

And then he grips my ankles, raising my legs in the air so that my red butt is off the mattress. Spreading my legs wide, he steps forward, and his cock slides into me. My neck arches back, as my eyes close, and I groan.

As he thrusts in and out, his pace growing, I buck against him until our bodies resonate in harmony. Panting, I don't want this moment to end, ever.

Then, as we reach a pace fast enough to power a car, Manuel moans loudly, as he throws his head back. His cock fully in me, he releases his warm cum.

My fingers dig into the bedspread, as my body stills, and another intense wave of pleasure washes over me.

As my body floats down from the orgasm, I think, *I love a man who knows there is pleasure in pleasing a woman as she would like. There is a God.*

***

I rest against Manuel's body, as he spoons me, his arm wrapped around my hip, his semi-erect cock pressing against a butt cheek. His post-sex cum soothes my burning butt.

He sits up on an elbow, looks down at me. "Caitlyn, I want this to be something more than just a fling."

My heart melts. "I want that too. But...but what about..."

"Liliana?"

I nod.

"Don't worry about Liliana. I will talk to her. She may be hesitant to accept at first, but she wants me to be happy. And she wants you to be happy too. She'll come around."

I caress his wrist. "I hope so."

He squeezes my hand. "And I want you to be happy, to not be...lonely."

I turn over to face him, and his deep brown eyes stare down as me. "Thank you," I say, "thank you Manuel."

Give Me All Your Love

Daryl appeared like an angel. As the snow fell in thick flakes, he waved both arms up and down at me while approaching my car, its back tires hopelessly encased in an ice-laden ditch. He motioned for me to roll down my window.

"I thought it was you, Norma," he said, as my face came into view and the warm air escaped into the cold. His espresso brown eyes twinkled. "Put it in neutral."

Without waiting for my response, he went back to his pickup truck, backed it up, then hooked a chain from it to my front axle. He jumped back into the truck. *Isn't he even going to ask me if I'm in neutral or not?* I wondered as his pickup pulled my car toward the shoulder. *Typical Daryl, just does what he wants. No wonder we don't date anymore.* My car fishtailed a little but in another second was out of the ditch. *But he is...effective.*

He unhooked the chain and came back to my window. "I usually charge $25 for that," he said once my window rolled down.

"How about a beer instead?" I said.

"Oh, the college girl has started drinking," he said, faux impressed. "Are you sure that's safe with me, the ex-high school boyfriend?"

I smirked. "I'm certain it's not, but I'm a big girl now and can take care of myself."

He glanced back at the tire tracks my car made across the ice patch and through the ditch. A sly grin twitched his lips. "Yes, I'm sure you can."

"It's either a beer or you're a Good Samaritan."

His eyebrow rose. "Well, I can't have people thinking the latter."

I grinned.

"Stagger Inn okay?"

"I'm right behind you."

He sauntered back to his truck, his boots leaving prints in the thickening snow. Damn, he had a good backside.

***

A wave of heat, the heady smell of beer, and the sparkle of Christmas lights hit me when we entered the Stagger Inn. We stomped the snow off our feet and each took a bar stool.

"Got your fake ID, Norma?" Daryl said, pulling his stocking cap off his mop of brown hair.

"It's Nori. What makes you think I'd have one?"

"*Nori?* Changed your name, did you? Is that what it says on your fake ID?"

"It's a nickname they gave me in the dorm, and I kinda like it. I bet you don't even show an ID."

Daryl shook his head, as if that was obvious. Of course not, he was a local and given the time his dad spent at the Stagger Inn, a legacy. He flashed two fingers at the bartender.

When the bartender arrived with our bottles, I pulled out my fake ID. He glanced at it and nodded. It always worked.

Daryl grabbed it out of my hand before I could stuff it back in my wallet. "Hey, this says you're two years older than me. Didn't tell me that when we were dating."

I swiped it back from him and set a ten on the bar. "Who are you seeing these days, Daryl?"

"I'm flattered you think I would be dating anyone at all. Not after the way you made me out to be when we broke up."

Yeah, I was a little harsh, I suppose. "What, all the sophomore girls at the high school taken?"

He snickered at that. "I only go for older women."

"All the junior girls taken then?"

He suppressed a grimace and tipped his beer at me in mock salute. Took that joke too far, I guess.

"Well thank you for stopping," I said. "I really appreciate it."

Daryl nodded, as I gazed at him. *He looks good,* I thought, *even better than when I dated him.*

"So, how do you like college over in Ames?" he said.

Ah, small talk time.

***

I grabbed my gut as giving a belly-aching laugh at Daryl's latest story. Somehow small talk turned into five hours, a half-dozen beers, and a move to a booth.

After we quieted, Daryl gazed straight into my eyes with a slight grin. "So, *Nori,* you've never told me – any boyfriends at the big college?"

"Would you be jealous?"

"So there *is* someone."

No, there hasn't been anyone. Not anyone at all.

"Maybe," I said.

"You're lying. There's no one."

I gave a faux expression of shock. "What makes you think that?"

"You're always lying when you answer 'maybe.'"

I blushed. *Well, now he knows…*

"So, that means you're still a …"

"A what?" I said.

"You know what."

"Can't say it?"

"Apparently you can't."

He was right, I couldn't. It was nothing I should be ashamed of, I knew, yet…

"Saving yourself for the right man," he said. "I can respect that."

I did a double-take. "That's surprisingly refreshing, Daryl."

"Especially coming from me, I bet."

"You pressured me enough."

His laughter drowned out the jukebox for a moment and rolled off the tavern's rafters. "Not *enough* obviously. Nori, I'll give you credit – you never were a tramp."

I sat there uncomfortably for a moment. Sex wasn't why we broke up – me going to college and the gulf that created was the reason – but it still felt like unfinished business between us.

"Hey," the bartender called over to us.

We looked up.

"Gonna close early," he said. "Snow is starting to pile up."

Daryl nodded and stood. *Guess it's time to go home.*

I rose. "Thanks again for rescuing me."

He canted his head at the table. "Thanks for the beers."

For a moment, we stood there awkwardly, facing one another.

"It was good to see you again, Norm–...Nori." He held out his arms.

We hugged, but I didn't let myself sink into him.

"You too," I said.

We had to push the tavern's door hard against the newly fallen snow. The white blinded me. I squinted, saw my car half-buried in snow.

"Oh Jesus, I'll never get home in this," I said.

"I can get you there," he said.

The snow was barely a quarter of the way up his pickup's tires. No doubt he had four-wheel drive too. "Okay."

"I'll come back when the storm is over and dig out your car."

"That would be great of you, thanks."

We climbed into the truck. It was high, almost like standing on a mountain vista. The truck roared to life, and he easily backed out. I resisted the temptation to slide over next to him like I used to.

In moments, we were on the highway, the windshield

wipers thwapping, heat from the vent filling the cab. Though there was no traffic on the road, it was still slow going.

We soon reached the turn to my parents' house. The road headed up a hill, one buried in a foot of snow, probably with a layer of ice beneath it, the same layer that sent my car into the ditch.

"Um, I don't think I can make it up that," he said, as we sat in the turn lane, staring at the snow drifts leading to Sieverding Ridge.

Wow, maybe Daryl has *grown up,* I thought. He never would have admitted that when we were dating. He would have turned and churned his way up it until getting stuck and angry.

"I can take you to a hotel back on the–" he started.

"No, I don't have the money," I said. *This time I won't say* maybe.

"How about to your Uncle Fre–"

"Your apartment is pretty close?" I quick said.

Daryl examined me for a moment. "Sure."

He continued driving. Though at the bar he spoke proudly of his first place of his own, I was sure it would be a dump. I didn't care. Heck, I lived in a door room smaller than his pickup.

***

His apartment wasn't half-bad actually. Just a kitchen with a short bar doubling as dining room table, a living room and two doors off it, one I bet for the bedroom, the other for the bath. The kitchen appliances looked like hand-me-downs from his parents, and the couch definitely was; we'd made out on it in his parents' den dozens of times.

"Hungry?" he said as I looked around.

I nodded. Must be a half-eaten sub sandwich somewhere in that old fridge, I figured.

Daryl pulled a sauce pan from a kitchen cupboard and started filling it with tap water.

"What're you doing?"

"Making spaghetti."

"When did you learn to cook?"

"When I discovered McDonald's was more expensive than buying groceries."

I watched him bring the water to a boil then measure out enough noodles for each of us. He dumped a jar of sauce into a smaller pot.

"You're pretty good at this," I said.

"Not so good that I didn't forget to turn on the oven for the garlic bread."

"Ooh, garlic bread, you are indeed a true chef. Got any bread?"

"Yeah."

"Stick it in the toaster. Where do you keep your spices?"

He pointed to the cupboard cattycorner to the toaster.

I rummaged through the cupboard, as he placed bread into the toaster. The warmth of his body washed over me as we stood so close. Hmmm...salt, pepper, steak seasoning, crushed red peppers, his body's sandalwood scent, bingo...garlic powder.

I handed it to him. "Sprinkle this on the toast after you butter it."

"How'd you know I had garlic?"

"Because your mom always had garlic powder, and I figured she stocked your cupboard as well as the rest of your house."

Daryl grinned as opening the refrigerator. "You know me pretty well." He placed a package of raw ground hamburger on the counter, and I grimaced.

"What?"

"I'm a vegetarian."

"You *weren't* last summer." He stuck the hamburger back in the fridge.

"Going vegetarian for me? I'm impressed."

"You've always impressed me."

"And who is trying to impress you these days?"

His face reddened. "No one really."

"Oh come on, with your muscles and killer brown eyes? Someone is after you."

"Well, Cristal has been awful flirty."

"Cristal Chambers? Oh God, you can do better than that." For personal reputation alone, I hoped she wasn't my...*replacement*.

"There's nothing to it. She's just a flirt. And what about you? Surrounded by all of those horny college boys, I bet you're on a date every night."

I blushed. "There's been a few dates. Nothing serious." I thought to the couple of times that dates swatted me on the butt when we were playing around, and the warm sensation I got between my legs whenever they did. Maybe I could get Daryl to do that.

He dumped the spaghetti into a strainer and dished up two plates. I took care of the garlic toast.

"Mmm, not bad," I said after my first bite.

"Thanks." Then he chuckled.

"What?"

"I was thinking of that hokey Disney film you made me watch, the one with the two dogs eating spaghetti."

I laughed. "*Lady and the Tramp.* It was a quite romantic scene."

As we ate, we picked up the conversation where we left off at the Stagger Inn. It flowed effortlessly, weaving in and out of laughter. For a moment, I had a vision, a vision that this could be the two of us, forever.

I gently brushed my foot against his leg and watched his reaction. He just kept eating and started talking about trucks, hunting and fishing.

So I lightly touched the tip of sock-clad foot against his ankle as maintaining eye contact. Gradually, my foot pressed slightly firmer.

No reaction. Just more about how he shot a buck earlier that month.

Time to go for broke. I circled my toe against his calf.

Taking in his last bite, he pulled back in his chair. *Guess he isn't interested.*

Then he rose, keeping his plate low, hiding his crotch, as he headed to the sink. *Well, maybe a little interested.*

I followed him to the sink with my plate.

"Wanna watch that movie again?" he said.

"You hated that movie."

"Being with you made it bearable. Besides, I owe you after talking about hunting and fishing through half of dinner."

"True enough."

We headed to the sofa, and he played with the remotes. He couldn't get a connection though.

"Lousy satellite dish never works when it snows." He tossed the remote to the coffee table, the same one I'd for years seen *House Beautiful* magazines artfully arranged upon but that now sported one chipped edge.

Our eyes locked for a long moment, then I looked away, trying not blush.

"We made a lot of good memories on this couch, didn't we?" he said.

I blushed. "There were a couple of memories we never got around to making."

"Say, Nori, why we didn't we ever do it when we were together?"

Good question. We almost did it once when we were going steady, but I didn't because I knew we had no contraception. "I wasn't properly motivated."

He ran his hand down my arm, barely touching me, and I shivered. "Let me see if I can motivate you now."

I scooted closer, and he wrapped his large arm around me, pulling me into a cuddle. I inhaled his sandalwood scent, the one I'd enjoyed for three years, and his lips lightly kissed my neck, working their way up from the shoulder to my ear. I closed my eyes and murmured. His lips moved to mine, and just as the tingle had almost dissipated from my neck, his lips returned to it.

Heart pounding, I tugged at the buttons on his denim shirt. Daryl more deftly unbuttoned my blouse, and once loose, I shook out of it. His hands circled around to my back, unclasped the bra, then gripping the front of it between its two cups, he pulled it downward. I'd finally opened the front of his shirt then scratched my nails down his bare abs.

His head fell back as he moaned. "Stand up," he said.

When I did, his fingers popped the top button of my pants open. The zipper descended and then so did my jeans and in short order my panties.

He rose as I sat down and exchanged the favor. When he stepped out of the puddle of his clothes, my fingers traveled over the contours of his muscles then down to his member, it engorged and erect. *Is this what a lady does*, I asked myself, *give you all my love?*

Daryl snuggled up next to me on the sofa, and his hand cupped and squeezed a breast as our lips locked again. His lips were warm and our tongues eager. The palm of his free hand went to the back of my neck, where his fingers softly tousled my hair and caressed the skin. Then his hand trailed up from my breast to the side of my face, gently stroking the jawline and neck.

My mind spun dizzily, as we each pulled up for air. An instant later, he lightly pressed his lips against mine again, planting butterfly kisses on them then the cheek and chin. The tip of his tongue slowly ran over my lips. My heaving breasts pressed against his bare chest, as I moaned.

The tip of his tongue unhurriedly entered my parted mouth then pulled back and re-entered. He repeated this motion, sometimes teasing me by holding back his tongue, but gradually increasing his speed until our tongues entwined in a mad dance. His hand at the back of my neck pulled the hair at the roots, tilting my head back, and I moaned again.

He returned to teasing me, as he softly nibbled my lips, gently licking and biting the curves on the upper lip then moving to the corners of the mouth, and just below the bottom lip. I pressed closer to him, pushing my hard nipples into him. As he inhaled, I exhaled, and our breathing synchronized.

Then he tugged on my lips, one at a time, and when my tongue reached for his mouth, he slowly and firmly sucked and released mine. He was pulling out every move we'd discovered together in high school, and for a moment I wondered why I'd ever given up on him.

As our tongues found one another again, every muscle in my body tensed. My nails dug hard into his back, and I let out a long groan. The whole world spun.

I pulled back, trying to catch my breath. "Oh my...God, I...just...came."

He held me close in his arms, letting me return to earth as basking in his warmth and sandalwood scent.

"I think someone might still have feelings for me," Daryl said. He pulled me over his lap. "And you've been a naughty girl for keeping it secret."

He smacked my bare butt.

I squealed as my calves flew up. "And you think this is

going to me to sleep with you?"

His palm slapped my ass again, and I yelped. My whole body tingled, and I found myself surprised, pondering how something painful could also be so...*tantalizing.*

"You deserve a spanking for all of those nasty things you said to me when we broke up," he said. His hand smacked my bare bottom again, and I let go a whimper of pleasure.

Daryl's fingers caressed my wet pussy lips as the sting of his swats vanished.

I wanted more. "Stopping already?"

"Oh you liked that, did you?"

His palm came down hard on my ass again, and I shrieked.

Daryl paused for a moment and gazed at me. I could only imagine the look of desire on his face. Then in one swoop he wrapped his arms around my legs and waist and stood, picking me up.

"Whoa," I giggled, as he carried me to the bedroom, his erect cock poking against my tummy, and tossed me onto the bed.

"Lay on your tummy and spread your legs," he said firmly.

I did. "Finally, you're properly motivating me to lose my virginity," I teased.

"So you've wanted to lose your virginity to me all that time, but you were holding out. You need to be disciplined, not motivated."

He gently stroked my bare butt, and the red-hot pain

cooled under the softness of his hand. I murmured my approval.

"You won't be groaning in pleasure in a moment or two," he said.

My fingers gripped the sheets in anticipation.

Daryl swatted my ass hard, and like a knee jerk my body jumped at the pain. I squealed as he gave each cheek a loud, stinging slap. My heart surged, as a warmth spread through my body.

He delivered another swat, and the pain lingered. I tightened my grip on the sheets.

Then he gave one more swat and then another in quick succession. I gasped. But I couldn't tell if it was from the pain or...

...*the pleasure.*

He paused a moment, rubbed my burning ass cheeks, giving me time to contemplate it –was I actually enjoying this? Did that make me a...*tramp?*

Then his hand descended with a searing force, this time harder than the last. I winced and found myself crying softly. He hit one butt cheek then the next, letting the burn ease in one then returning it so the pain would rise again.

My body trembled.

His free hand held the back of my thigh just below my ass, keeping me in place. My heart beat faster; no this isn't supposed to be enjoyable, I told myself, yet I grinded against the mattress and gasped with each new swat.

"Hey, what's this?" he said and pulled his hand from

my thigh. "My palm, it's wet!"

He stopped spanking me, looked at my thigh, almost certainly saw a trickle of my juices running down it from my pussy. Most of it had soaked the sheets beneath my wet lips.

"Why you little–" he said.

He didn't have to say it. I knew him well enough. I was a little tramp. *His* little tramp.

His hand pressed me mid-back, and he swatted again and again. God I wished he would stop, wished he would put his finger in me.

But he didn't have to, for with each smack his palm laid on my ass, my body grew taut until I screamed, and my whole body shook. Panting from the orgasm, I collapsed against the mattress, let its softness catch me.

Daryl stood there for a moment, watching me come down from my second high of the evening. At last he said, "Lift your butt into the air."

Now that's the Daryl I know. I shifted so I was on my knees, but my torso and face were on the bed. I was too exhausted to do more.

Daryl got on the bed behind me, rubbed his cockhead against my slit. It easily slipped in, and he took my virginity. I felt a slight discomfort but moaned, as he slowly slid in and out of me. I'd never felt so full then groaned as my muscles slowly tensed. He always was so...*effective.*

I bucked against him, urging him to go faster. He stopped thrusting, and my hips took over, riding his cock, taking in more of it with each thrust. His hand grabbed my butt cheek and pressed down, holding me in place, and he took over, thrusting madly.

My eyes glazed over. "Yes..." I mewled and gripped the bedsheets.

Then with one last deep thrust, his hands tightened on my hips, and he growled, cumming inside me. As his cock throbbed, releasing his warm seed, my body suddenly tightened then quivered over and over in orgasm beneath him.

***

Daryl fell onto the bed beside me, and I rolled over, resting my head on his chest and draping a leg across his, as he wrapped an arm around me. I could make out my red juices on his cock, it now at half-mast. A glow and enormous smile covered our faces.

"I wonder how long the snowstorm is supposed to last," I said after a few moments.

"At least through the night. Looks like your stuck again." He squeezed my shoulder.

I chuckled. "Maybe this time I want to be stuck – and with you at that."

"Just *maybe*? Maybe you still think I'm not safe to be with."

I smirked. "You may not be, but I'm a big girl now and can make my own decisions."

He patted my shoulder. "And I'm glad you did; I'm very glad you did."

Me too.

Hurts So Good

My jaw dropped. "How much?"

"About $5000. It's a particularly nasty accusation your husband has made."

"It's not true, though."

My divorce attorney, Alan Wagner, leaned forward, his broad shoulders stretching wide beneath his shirt. "We can win, I assure you, Nancy. His strategy, though, appears to be to run your bank account dry so that you have no choice but to give in."

And Daren's strategy is working. "I've spent every dime I have. I thought we were done with this."

Alan's blue eyes glinted, as he contemplated me for a moment. "There must be a family member you can borrow from. Maybe a close friend?"

I shook my head. "I've already borrowed as much as I can. Please don't give up on me yet."

He gazed a few seconds at the far corner of the room. "Maybe we can work something out. Unfortunately, I need to get to court right now." He scribbled something on a piece of a stationery and handed it to me. "Meet me here for dinner tonight, and we'll talk some more. In the meantime, see if someone in your family is willing to help out."

I looked at his note: *Victoria's on 1st Ave., 6pm.*

"Victoria's? If I can't afford you, I surely can't afford to eat there."

He waved his hand dismissively as standing. "My treat tonight."

I stood as well. "Thank you, Alan. That's very kind of you." *I hope he didn't mind me calling him Alan.*

He nodded. "Make some calls, okay?"

"I will."

***

I sat in the recliner, the same one I'd made love to Daren in plenty of times, though now it was in my one-bedroom apartment and not our house. Sometimes when we were first married, I'd wait naked for him in that chair until he got home, and when he finally came through the door, I'd smile seductively at him and slowly run my hand over a breast.

He'd drop his coat and briefcase on the floor, cup my cheeks and kiss me. My hands tangled in his black curls, pulling him closer, never getting enough. Then my hands wrapped around his enticing broad shoulders, poised elegantly in a very professional gray suit. The jacket would be the first thing I'd strip, followed quickly by the white button-up shirt tucked into his trim waist. I didn't care if he left on the dark blue tie; we could find several uses for it once we were naked.

Then he'd stand and rapidly pull down his pants and the boxers underneath, and with his thick cock bobbing in front of him, he'd grab my ankles and pull me to him, enter in one quick thrust. I squealed, as he took me, using me for his own pleasure.

I always found something sexy about a decisive, confident man, of giving into him like a yielding sacrifice who knew she served a greater purpose. I soon discovered that the best way to get Daren to take control was to make him think that you'd do anything for him. And I would.

Then came the day when my hand dipped under his waistband. We hadn't had sex in a week. He squirmed out of my embrace, pushed my hand back when it went for his jean's top snap.

I stood there, waiting for him to do something utterly surprising to me.

And then he did just that. "You know, sometimes I'm tired and just not in the mood," he said and walked to the den, shutting the door behind him.

He ignored me when I cried.

***

My high heels clacked against the sidewalk, as I made my way toward Victoria's entrance. I'm sure if anyone had seen me get out of my beat up car, they would have been surprised to spot a woman wearing a lowcut red dress that accentuated a terrific ass. Surely a woman who could pull that off would have some guy fulfilling all of her needs, including getting her a decent vehicle. I thought Daren was that guy. It wasn't my first mistake in life but certainly the worst.

I wondered if I was making another one.

Heading straight to the maître d', before I could change my mind I quickly said, "I'm here to meet Alan Wagner."

"He is seated and expecting you. Follow me."

Alan rose, smiling with his dimples and glittering blue eyes, as soon as he caught sight of us. His sandy blond hair appeared darker in the dim light. "You sure make that dress look beautiful," he said.

I blushed, as the maître d' seated then handed me a menu.

We made small talk for a while, as if avoiding something. All the while, I noticed other couples leaving and being seated. A jealous tinge colored my thoughts; I hadn't had good sex in a long while, not even the last year that Daren and I were together.

Finally, after our main course arrived, Alan leaned forward. "Did you have any luck with your family?"

I shook my head. I made calls but had already tapped out every well. Most gave the advice to simply give in, that fighting wasn't worth it. Maybe they were right. Still, why should he win by lying? My eyes went to the floor. "I've already borrowed money from everyone. But I don't...want to give up."

He nodded. "I'm sure we could work something out. But before we agree to anything, I must warn you – in court, you will have to do everything I tell you. And you may also need to make some...sacrifices."

The way he said *sacrifices* sent a tingle through me.

Alan gazed at me as if trying to judge just what I'd be willing to accept. I suppose he'd done the same with countless juries so he could save his client.

My turn to see precisely what he had in mind. "Could we do a monthly payment plan?"

The corners of his lips crinkled. "If your ex fights, we'll most likely have to go with that. For the moment, though, we need to concern ourselves with the retainer fee so I can answer his false accusations."

I nodded and waited for him to elaborate. For a long moment, his steel blue eyes gazed at me. His arms strained against his suit, but it didn't appear to fit tight; rather it nicely highlighted his attributes. I checked his ring finger, as I had the first time we met, and like then there was no band or light-colored skin where one had been. Then I chuckled. I always found it ironic that a man who'd never married was a divorce attorney.

"Look, Alan, I'm not dumb. I know what you're suggesting."

His eyebrow rose quizzically. "You only have to do what you're willing to do."

"It's just a matter of negotiating the price then."

He paused and eyed me again. "You're a beautiful woman, Nancy. Frankly, I don't understand why your husband is doing this; in my opinion, he's an idiot to give you up. I've never made this arrangement before with any woman. But you're...irresistible."

I grinned. "Do you really expect me to believe a lawyer?"

He smiled. "Touché. For my retaining fee, you spend tonight with me, and we go all the way."

"That covers the whole five grand?"

"Yes."

"And if *I* don't orgasm, you'll give me an additional thousand dollars of billable hours free."

His smile stretched from ear to ear. "You should have been an attorney, Nancy. Your negotiation skills are excellent. All right, deal – on one condition. I get to cum inside you, no condom, or you've only covered $4000 of the retaining fee."

"Now I know *you* really are an attorney."

He raised his glass of wine. "Deal?"

I tinked his glass with mine. "Deal."

***

The day after I cried, I waited naked for Daren in the recliner. Makeup sex? Maybe. Trying to rekindle what we once had? Definitely.

When he finally came through the door, I parted my lips and smiled, as slowly running my hand over a breast.

Daren placed his coat in the closet. "Really, Nancy? Now?" He took his briefcase to the kitchen.

I sprung from the chair, my hands balled into fists, and followed him. "Why aren't you interested in me anymore?"

His eyes widened with righteous indignation. "Look, work has been very stressful."

I pressed against his back, ran a hand from his chest down to his cock, as he poured himself a glass of water from the tap. "Maybe you need something to help you relax."

He pushed me away with his elbow. "Jesus, Nancy, not *now*."

I rolled my eyes. "Maybe you need some Viagra."

His face firmed, and he grabbed both of my arms. My

eyes widened. His mouth came to mine, as he forced his tongue inside me. My heart quickened, and my tongue reciprocated.

And then he spun me around so I faced the edge of the kitchen island. One hand gripped my arm above the elbow and the other pressed my upper back downward so I was bent over it. He quickly unzipped his trousers, rubbed against me. My hips gyrated in kind, then his cock plunged into me.

I grabbed the island's side with my free arm as he pistoned into me. He pulled my held arm behind my back, tightened his hold on it.

"Is this what you want?" he said, as thrusting faster than my hips could meet his cock.

My fingers gripped the island tighter, and I wished he'd finish.

And then with one last slam, he growled and came inside me. A moment later, he let go of my arm and withdrew from me.

"*There.* Satisfied now?" he sneered.

With that, he went to the den.

***

After desert at Victoria's, I climbed into the passenger seat of Alan's BMW X5 – which I swear was nicer than my apartment – and he drove through the spring night to his place.

"I'm glad we were able to get together tonight," he said. "I've been thinking a lot about you lately."

I grinned at him. "And what have you been thinking?"

"They haven't all been dirty thoughts, trust me. I just

thought getting to know you better would be nice."

"So there were *some* dirty thoughts?"

His blush showed, as we passed under a street light. "Yes."

"That's good then."

His townhouse was in the Biltmore area, the doorway framed in palms, a heated pool that steam rose off as the desert night cooled. Once inside, he gestured toward the sofa. "Drink?"

I smiled. "Why not?"

He went to a bar off the side of the room, opened a cabinet. "What's your pleasure?"

"Sloe gin and fresh orange juice?"

A moment later, he handed me the drink and sat on the sofa. "Is there anything I should know for tonight?"

I slowly shook my head. "I've been faithful to Daren since we started dating 12 years ago."

He smiled. "Work keeps me busy. I've not been in a relationship for a few years."

"I find that hard to believe."

"Then I'm glad you're not on a jury in any of my cases."

"So long as there's nothing that I should know, I'm not worried about your relationships."

"There isn't. Is there anything you don't like? Or anything that your husband did that would remind you of him?"

Hmm, very considerate. I thought on it for a moment. "Unless you plan to ignore me in bed tonight, I'm sure I won't mix up the two of you."

"He clearly didn't appreciate you. That's a shame."

My gaze dipped to the carpeted floor. I thought about that woman's shaking legs wound around Daren's waist, rocking softly with each gentle plunge, as he fucked her on our bed when I came home early one day from work. His smug smile as he looked over his shoulder hit me with full force.

That other woman – Janessa or Janella or Janice or something like that – *took charge*, he said, as we shouted at one another afterward. He was tired of always being the one who directed the show.

Alan brought me back to the present. "He must be very angry at you to do this."

I wanted a man whose passions left him with no control, who could not help but dominate me, I realized. Anger was not the kind of dominance I sought at all. Anger was oppression; dominance arising from passion meant knowing how to take control and please me while you pleased yourself.

"He's not angry," I said. "He's just trying to hurt me."

***

I crashed my face into Alan's chest, and wrapping my arms around him cried and cried and cried. He held me, soothing my back and the crown of my head.

Then, as he buried a caressing hand into my long hair, his other hand tilted my head up, and he placed a tender kiss upon my lips. I closed my eyes to relish the dangerous intensity. Encouraged, he trailed his lips down my neck and elicited a traitorous moan from me. My pulse raced, and I felt lightheaded, as if about to collapse.

At that moment, I wanted Alan more than anything in the entire world.

My finger traced the curve of his arm as I spoke. "Perhaps I could do some additional work for you tonight...for some additional discounts?"

He played with my hair. "I'm betting you have something in mind."

A devilish grin slowly crossed my face. "I might."

"I'm amenable to your proposal."

"Excellent. Sit back on the sofa." As he did, I stood over his knees. *I can take charge too and please a man.*

Leaning my chest into his face with the butt slightly out, I gingerly lowered myself onto his lap. Moving my hips in a slow circular motion, I made direct eye contact with him. I breathed in the woody, floral musk of his scent. His hands reached for my arms, but I shook my head, and he put them back at his side. *Good boy.*

Wrapping arms around his neck, my hips closed on his torso. His half-erect cock met me, our clothes a barrier, and as I gyrated on his lap, it grew tall and firm against my dress.

I quick grazed my lips against his. His hand cupped the back of my head, and I when my lips went in for a quick brush, he held me in place as our mouths locked. His tongue pressed its way past my lips, and then entwined with mine. *Even better, boy.*

My hips rose slightly, and my wet slit slid up and down the front of his pants, as I gyrated.

His large hands squeezed my butt cheeks, as I rubbed

his cock. "You've got a nice ass, Nancy. So perky…"

I pulled back a little fearing he'd cum. "How much was that worth, Mr. Wagner?"

He shrugged. "Say $50?"

My finger drew circles over his muscular upper arm. "That's very generous. I'm glad to see you weren't bored."

"Turn around," he said.

Finally, he wants to take charge. I sat backward on his lap, his hard cock pressing through his pants into my back.

***

Arriving home early, I wondered if I might convince Daren over a homemade dinner to bed me. We needed to connect again, relight what we once had.

The soft murmur of groans and grunts greeted me as I entered the apartment. Was he masturbating? *Ooh, my chance!*

Stepping into the bedroom doorway, there before me was a woman's shaking legs wound around his waist, rocking softly with each gentle plunge, as he fucked her on our bed. He didn't stop. His smug smile as he looked over his shoulder hit me with full force.

I screamed.

The woman laying beneath Daren pushed him off, and with eyes wide stared at me. A moment later, she jumped off the bed and grabbed her clothes.

My raised arm pointed to the door. "Get the fuck out of here, whoever you are."

As she scrambled to dress, I left then stood in the

living room, as my blood boiled. When I heard her pass and the door close behind me. I grabbed the vase on the mantle and marched toward the bedroom.

Daren was pulling on his pants, having a difficult time getting it over his still engorged cock, the cock that had just been inside another woman. I threw the vase at him, and he ducked. An instant later, it smashed against the walls, leaving a shard of green glass on the bed.

"Who the hell was that?" I shouted.

"Nancy, I can explain–"

"There's nothing to explain, I saw it with my own eyes. You said you were overworked, that you were tired."

"I *am* tired," he said, as pulling a shirt over his head.

"Looked like you had a lot of energy a few minutes ago. What the hell, am I not good enough anymore? I'm your wife!"

"Janessa loves me with a passion you've never shown. She *takes charge.*"

"And it sure looked like you were enjoying the ride!"

He sneered. "You're fucking boring, Nancy! You just let me do whatever I want."

"*Most* men would like that."

"What I'd like is for you to show how much *you* want me."

"Don't I when I let you do whatever you want?"

He rolled his eyes and went to the closet. Pulling a suitcase from it, he set it on the bed.

I yanked it toward me. "No, you stay here. I'm the one who's leaving. I'll never be able to sleep in that bed again." I went to the chest of drawers, started grabbing my clothes from it.

"Don't make this difficult, Nancy. We can work through this."

"There's *nothing* to work through."

"If you leave, Nancy, there's no coming back."

I laughed. "I'll pick up the rest of my stuff tomorrow when you're at work. Don't be here."

His face twisted up. "You'll regret this, Nancy."

Latching the suitcase, I grasped its handle and headed to the front door. "The only thing I'll ever regret is having met you."

***

My head pressed against Alan's shoulder, as I moaned. One of his hands squeezed a breast; his other had two fingers deep in my cunt.

Then his fingers arched up, as if making a come-hither motion, and slowly rubbed back and forth across the top of vaginal walls, as if searching for something.

What felt like an electric shock sparked through me, as my neck flew back. He'd found something. My G-spot.

He must have noticed my reaction, for he kept rubbing there. My breathing deepened, and my fingers gripped his thighs. Ripples of growing pleasure swept through my body, as I grew close.

His hand on my breast flicked then squeezed its hardening nipple, and my fingernails dug into his thighs. My hips rode his fingers; my bare ass slid along his engorged cock.

And then my muscles clenched around his fingers

like a vice, as I arched up. I let go a loud groan, and my body froze for a long moment then slumped against him.

"That was so hot," he said. "You've just saved yourself a thousand dollars."

I turned my face to him, and our lips meet. His kiss seared my lips, all hot desire and urgency. I had to catch my breath again. "How else...can I...please you?" I said.

"Stand up."

Ah, he wants me on my knees, giving him a blow job, I thought. I could do that before we crawled into bed and he had his way with me. So I stood, despite my lightheadedness and wobbly knees.

But when he did as well, there was no unsnapping of his belt buckle and trousers puddling around his feet. Instead, he walked to the umbrella stand by his front door and pulled a walking cane from it.

"I've always admired your perfectly round ass, Nancy," he said. "I'll take a hundred dollars off the bill for each time you let me strike it."

I swallowed hard. "With that?" I'd had spankings before, but never with a cane. Given how well he'd treated me so far, I couldn't imagine he'd hurt me.

He nodded. "As I said earlier, you only have to do what you're willing to do."

There was something so sexy about him standing there, in control, in authority. I imagined all the times he was in a courtroom, holding the fate of a man or woman in his hands. The outline of his cock bulged at his pants front. Despite the cane in his hand, somehow I felt safe, protected. He desired me, and so he wouldn't hurt me.

"Okay, let's try it," I said softly.

He tapped the walking cane against a wall with a low bookcase against it. "Come over here and bend over."

I slowly walked to the wall, stood by it.

"Take your dress off."

I unzipped it at the back, let it fall to my ankles.

He ran the cane along the back of my leg. "And the panties."

I hesitated.

"Go ahead," he said.

Pulling them past my knees, I let gravity take them to the floor. The thin lace wasn't going to much protect my skin anyway.

He tapped the top of the bookshelf. "Place your hands there."

I set my palms on the hard oak. My butt jutted out a bit.

He stood there for a long moment, admiring my ass, probably wondering why Daren wasn't begging for it. He had, at first.

Thwack!

I jumped as his cane struck both of my butt cheeks. A sharp and quick burning sensation hung on my skin. He let the cane linger there against my ass, as the sting dissipated. Then he pulled it away.

Thwack!

He struck my butt again, this time lower. The cane remained there as my knees wobbled; this time the sting lingered.

Then he pulled the cane back. An instant later, its wicked hiss sounded then came the awful *crack* as it seared my bare flesh.

My lower leg bent up, as I danced in place a moment. He pulled the cane away this time and waited until I settled down.

Thwack!

I jumped, but this time his strike was not as hard. Was he getting bored?

Thwack!

I yelped. That one was harder than any before.

He stepped back a moment, maybe admiring his handiwork. At least four of the strikes still burned, and I imagined there were long red lines across my bare ass.

Thwack!

My knees caved forward, but I kept my position, as my palms pressed harder against his bookshelf.

Thwack!

I jumped and danced again to loosen the sting. That one was his hardest yet. A tear formed in my eye. It wasn't the only place I was getting wet.

Thwack!

That one was lighter, and I breathed back in my snot.

He stepped back again. "That's $900 you've saved this evening. Shall we go for an even thousand?"

I remained silent, trying to decide if that question was rhetorical. He tapped my butt cheek with his cane.

"Or is that enough?"

I swallowed hard. "One more."

Thwack!

I grit my teeth. It was his hardest yet.

"Very well then, a thousand it is." He made to walk toward his umbrella stand.

"Hmm, that hurts...so good," I said as standing up, rubbing my behind. My juices dripped from my pussy onto my thigh.

He laughed and placed the cane back in the stand, then returning to me, forcefully grabbed the back of my neck. "There's a part of paying my retaining fee that I now need you to make good on." His other hand rested on my hip and guided me toward a hallway with a door at the end of it.

As we entered the door, a king-sized bed spread before us.

"I hope you're not tired," he said. "I plan to please you all night."

A swell of heat coursed through me. "The night is young, Alan." As my lips closed, I smiled seductively.

Sky High

The stronger, the better, I always say, and Mario proves my point. He finds a rock to grip and pulls himself up with that arm as lifting a leg to a new foothold, his muscles moving like cables under his skin. I refocus my attention to the cliff wall so I can reach the top with him. We're almost there, but the climbing guidebook warned that the section before the lip is difficult.

I glance back at him, as his other arm and leg negotiates the wall a few feet higher, and rationalize that if I get stuck then knowing how he got there would give me an alternate route to climb.

A whiff of his spiced aftershave drifts past, as he moves higher than me. I bring my hand up to find a new hold. Time to catch him.

***

Yes, time to catch him. That's what I told myself a week before, when I saw him for the first time practice climbing on a small cliff outside of town. He ascended the granite with ease, curly black hair flowing down to his chin in soft ringlets.

A guy like him wouldn't be humdrum or boring, I told myself. But you've got to be careful with men; they boast about being adventurous, yet the moment you suggest they prove it, they get all scared and make you feel ridiculous.

Moments later, he'd descended and detached himself from the belay device. Then he stopped and looked over his shoulder, clearly saw me staring at him. He grinned, and his emerald green eyes panned from my head to my toes. He nodded then returned to detaching his harness.

"Nice climb – your footwork was supercreative," I said. "I'm Summer by the way."

"Thanks. You looked pretty good yourself. I'm Mario."

I let his name linger on my brain for a moment too long and find myself unable to think of what to say next.

He saved me, motioned toward my gear. "Looks like you've been climbing for a while, Summer."

"I'm training for Big Moe."

He looked up at me, a curl of his hair wafting in the wind. "You're going to love that climb. Did it last year. It's great from bottom to top. You can free solo it."

"Cool. What're you climbing next...Mario?" I liked how his name rolled off my tongue.

"Stress Relief, over in Joshua Tree. Doing it next Saturday."

"Oh yeah? I've heard it's a challenge."

He nodded. "Good TTS. Say, want to climb it with me? It's got a fantastic view and would be great training for Big Moe."

No need to sell me on it with the great training bit.
"Sure. Who's all going?"

"Right now just you and me."
Perfect.

Worry lines crossed his forehead. "Is that all right?"

I smiled. "We'll have a great time."

***

Yes, a great time. I break into a sweat as seeking another handhold. There's no way I'm going to embarrass myself in front of him.

My fingertips find a hold, but I'll need a little more arm strength than I can garner to make this one. I pause a few seconds to ready my head for it. My arm extends all the way, then as my fingers grip the hold, I pull with every ounce of strength my willpower can coax. My other hand locates an easy break in the rock's side to plant itself while the toes clasp onto the slender knobs where my hands had been only moments ago.

I wonder if Mario saw me.

Glancing over at him, he's busy negotiating his portion of the cliff, seemingly off in his own world. That's probably for the best, actually; if you let your concentration slip, that's when mistakes are made, and mistakes are deadly. It's advice I should follow rather than peeking all the time at his body rippling with muscle.

I identify the next hold for my hand to grip. Never mind his body, this morning I put on my sexiest pair of black panties, and now they're crawling into the crack of my ass, and that alone makes concentrating a challenge.

Soon we're side by side. He scans the cliffside above him; it looks extremely smooth. So does my side, in truth. I notice some tiny gouge, and lift myself toward it.

There's hardly any sound at all, just the occasional squawk of some distant bird, the whistle of the wind when it did rise, and my soft huffs and puffs as I reach for the hold.

My fingers slip. I pull the belay rope to stop me, and just before it catches, a hand grabs my upper arm. Once my fingers and toes regrip the rock wall, Mario lets me go.

I glance up at him. He's clinging onto the wall with one hand and two feet. His other hand returns to a hold.

"Thanks," I said, the heat of the sun on my back.

"Your catch would have stopped you."

Maybe he was right in dismissing his part. What really mattered was that he instinctively tried to save me. Maybe he'd do that that for anyone and not because he felt strongly about me. Either way, did it matter?

***

Did it matter that he hardly texted me the week after we'd met? Just a request for where to pick me up and then, after my response, the time when he'd be there.

I danced a little jig knowing we'd see one another again. Men who engaged in risk taking – I don't mean stupid stuff like binge drinking and gambling but instead extreme sports like base jumping or glacier trekking – never disappointed in bed. They didn't want a moment of their lives to be humdrum or boring. I could get vanilla sex from any guy, but for a truly spectacular orgasm, one where your brain feels like it's on crack cocaine – there needed to be a certain sense of excitement, of danger even. Only men of adventure seemed to know how to achieve that when between the sheets.

Mario's silence, though, left me wondering if he even was interested. Maybe he really just wanted someone to climb a rock with. The buddy system was safe, after all.

I texted him. *How you doing?*

He responded, *Hey.*

Me: *I'm excited about our climb.*

Him: *It'll be a good challenge.*

I paused for a moment. He wasn't excited too?

Neither did he continue the conversation.

I let it go. He probably was busy.

Each day I'd text something new to him. His responses were short – not impolite, not a brush off, just short.

I started to doubt myself. Maybe I wasn't strong enough to climb this rock, and he realized that but thought backing out was too awkward. No, that's nonsense, I told myself. Maybe then I wasn't his type in the looks department, and he didn't want to encourage anything. No, I'm in good shape, I told myself, any guy would want to take a tumble in the hay with me.

Maybe he's a shallow guy. A lot of guys are just into lifting weights or doing some physical hobby like running or rock climbing over and over, their thoughts never going any deeper than the next step in whatever they were doing.

Just who was this man?

Well, I'll know soon enough, I decided, we're spending Saturday together climbing a rock. In the meantime, I needed to let it all go or I'd find myself drinking heavily to get some stress relief.

***

At Stress Relief's lip, my fingers reach the rock's top, and as if doing a push up I raise my body onto it. He offers a hand, and his arm steadies me as I lift my leg atop the rock.

"Ah, a gentleman!" I say.

I crawl a step away from the rim then slowly stand. The rock's top is flat with a knee-high boulder at its center, sitting there as if an altar. The uneven edges of the rock stand out.

"Wow, we're sky high," I say.

Mario grins as the light breeze tussles a curl of his hair, and he slinks out of his harness. "Nice climb. You've got great technique."

"Thanks. You weren't kidding about the great view. Look at that!"

A flat beige desert, punctuated with jumbles of monzogranite, spreads out all around us. Barren mountains, no longer green now that spring has ended, surround the valley floor. Not another person is in sight. Talk about good time to solitude, he wasn't kidding.

I lean into him to get close, but Mario stiffens – and not in the right place. After a second, he steps away.

Girlfriend. He must have a girlfriend. Stupid of me to not ask! On the other hand, he hadn't made searching for info about him easy either.

***

I searched for him on Facebook. Then LinkedIn. Then

98

Instagram. Then X and any other social media I could think of the day before our joint climb.

There wasn't much of a presence anywhere. Not like me with 2000+ pics on Instagram, and sometimes two or three daily posts on Facebook, and a LinkedIn profile that even included my high school activities. I didn't spend much time on X anymore – it had devolved into bots and political propaganda – but in its heyday when Twitter, I shared photos and updates there all the time.

I texted him about it. *Are you on any social media?* Might as well be point blank about it.

A while later, he responded, *Yeah but don't really use any. I'm not much into all the noise.*

Me: *Guess now you know I'm stalking you, lol*

A few minutes later came: *I presume you're wondering if I'm safe.*

I thought to myself that wasn't the impression I wanted to give at all. Though now that he mentions it, I probably should consider that.

So I typed: *Well are you?*

A moment passed. *I apologize for not texting more. I'm in a high-intensity job. I cut a lot out so I can focus and keep peace of mind.*

A high-intensity job? Yum, that sounded sexy. I typed: *What do you do?*

Him: *Criminal investigator*

"OK, he's safe," I said aloud.

I texted, *See you tomorrow morning. You're good.*

***

99

Mm-hmm, you are good looking, I think, as watching him standing there, his thick arms on his hips, as he stares across the valley floor. A hawk rides a thermal in the distance.

"What do we do now?" I say.

"Sit and relax." With that, he slowly lowers himself to the wind-smoothed ground and gazes out at the expansive desert. Why he didn't sit on the knee-high boulder baffles me, but that is his business.

I plop down next to him. We watch the hawk rise quickly, flapping its wings only occasionally. Then, hundreds of feet in the air, it glides off.

After a moment, I say, "I love watching you climb, you're so graceful."

"Thank you. You're quite good yourself."

He continues staring into the distance, so I do the same. Each line of the mountains in the range surrounding the valley carries its own swath of the color – the nearest one orange, the next one beige, and one beyond that white, it soft and harmonious, inherently warm.

"You're the quiet type, aren't you?"

He chuckles. "Quiet is why I come out here."

"So, are you seeing anyone?"

He shakes his head. "No, why?"

"Because…well, you're kind of standoffish to me."

His eyes soften. "I'm a quiet man, surrounded by noise all week. This is my opportunity to find peacefulness, to center myself."

"Oh." *Great, I'm just making things worse.*

"I don't mean to make you feel alone," he says. "Here. Let us do something together." He scoots on his butt to face my side, sits cross-legged, and motions for me to face him.

When I do, Mario holds out his hands. "Take them," he says gently.

My fingers touch his then slide forward to rest on his palms.

"Gaze into my eyes," he says.

I look into his pretty greens and he into my baby blues, and within moments the whole world quiets. There is just him and me in it; not even the teasing wind or sweltering sun seem to matter. A pattern of emerald rays emanate from his pupil, which a beige ring surrounds, and I sense that there is far more to him than just work and rock climbing, that inside him are thoughts and feelings I have yet to fathom.

Mario whispers, "Now listen to my breathing, and I will listen to yours. Let us try to breathe at the same rate."

Staring into his beautiful eyes, I slow my breathing to match his, as he increases to match mine. Soon our chests rise and fall at the same rhythm. My thoughts slow, smooth out as if a heavy metal band gradually transitioning from something up tempo to a soft ballad. The universe is so silent and consists only of us two.

I want to touch him everywhere, to know everything about him.

He withdraws his hands, and the synchronicity of our breathing fades.

"I'm seeking freedom," he says, as if he had read my mind, my desire to understand him. "I want the freedom to enjoy life, the freedom to drift in my thoughts, the freedom to be where I've never been before."

I long to be one with him again. "I wish to be free too."

Mario's eyebrows rise, as if asking me to explain.

I pull my shirt off over my head. "I wish to be naked where I've never been before." I unsnap the sports bra and let my breasts fall free, savor the warm air washing over my bare skin. Then I lean toward him and tug his shirt upward. He holds his arms high so I can draw it off him.

A moment later, he cups my face with one hand then kisses my neck with such softness, like the summer rains descending to sprinkle arid hills. My fingers explore his taut abs, as the rocking press of his mouth upon me steals my breath.

I slip my hand on top of his bulge, rub, and lick my lips. "Is this for me?"

***

His Jeep arrived for me exactly when he said it would. I'm out the door with all of my gear just as Mario headed up the walkway.

"Need any help?" he said.

"Sure." I handed him my rope and harness, which he carried with ease to the back of his Jeep.

We pulled out, an hour's drive from Joshua Tree, plenty of time to get to know one another. But his conversation was like his texts…he answered but said little more.

Maybe it's because I'm making small talk, I told myself. Who wants to discuss the weather and traffic anyway?

"Tell me more about what you do for a living," I said.

"Specialized Investigations Division. Over in San Bernardino."

"Sounds exciting."

"It can be. One moment you're on a child abuse case, the next you're on a murder."

"You said it was high intensity."

He nodded. "Families depend upon you to bring them answers about what happened to their loved ones. D.A.'s depend upon you to bring them evidence so they can file charges. There are a lot of cases. Staying on top of them and trying to be two places at once makes for a chaotic life most days."

Wow, that was the greatest number of words he'd strung together for me since we'd met. "Must be stressful."

"It is. What about you? What do you do?"

"I'm a naturalist over at the wildlife sanctuary in Redlands."

He nodded again. Guess I'd satisfactorily answered his question.

"It's involves a lot of monitoring," I add. "Walk the trails and count the plants and animal populations. Run a test on the water quality. That sort of thing."

"Sounds peaceful."

"It can be downright boring at times. You ever spend

a whole afternoon counting the number of black mustard plants are on a hillside?"

He seemed to look wistful for a moment then shook his head. "Can't say I have."

***

"Honestly, I can't say it *isn't*," Mario says about his erection on the top of Stress Relief. He unhurriedly takes off his climbing shoes then stands and takes down his pants. The fullness of his cock stretches and strains the black boxers beneath them.

"Well, look at that," I said, "we're wearing the same color." I stand as well, undo my harness and slip out of my pants.

I swear his cock twitched at the sight of my lace panties. Guess they were worth it after all.

Mario picks up his pants and tosses them at my feet. Just when I think he's going to demand that I get down on my knees and blow him – not that I'd mind – he drops to his knees and places his large hands on my thighs. His face is even with my pussy, and his teeth nimbly pull the panties to one side of my folds. An instant later, his tongue, hot and wet, separates my slit.

His tongue slips fully in, gradually sweeps up until its tip finds my clit, then he passes over it in slow, lazy circles, his warm breath sending shivers up the length of my body. I let go a small gasp and run my fingers through his dark hair.

Mario's tongue leaves my clit, but before I can give a disappointed groan, he kisses along my labia then gently pinches them with his lips. Then he's back to my

104

clit, those long, gentle circles around its sides. My heart beats faster and neck falls back, as his large hands caress my thighs and his tongue my hardening clit.

Then his whole mouth kisses my pussy, widens, and sucks it into his mouth. My eyes close as I moan.

His own pretty greens look up mischievously at me. He fingers the waistband of my panties. I arch my back and raise my hips for him, as he pulls the black lace below my knees, where it slips to the ankles.

Then he's back to working my clit, taking his time pleasing me, as if he's got all day to make me cum. And he does, of course, but I want to cum now, over and over, so my hips grind on his tongue, urging him onward.

He wraps one strong hand about the side of my waist and holds me in place, so I'm forced to go at his pace. My hips gyrate to his tongue, my bosom thrusting in and out, as my breathing deepens.

His tongue quick flicks sideways across my clit, sending my head into a sexual frenzy. My knees weakening, I hold on to his curly hair to steady myself.

Then his tongue flips my clit up and down, until I no longer know which direction the pleasure is coming from. Every muscle in my body tenses, and my nails dig into the crown of his head, as I scream. A moment later, I collapse onto him, and his large hands wrap around my back and ass, holding me up while I catch my breath.

A few minutes later, I dizzily step back. "Wow...that was fantastic."

A satisfied smirk covers his face. "I could tell."

"Oh?"

"That scream you gave when you came. I bet you could hear it across the entire desert valley."

***

At last we arrived at a desert valley within Joshua Tree National Park. The vast number of alien-looking plants – the park's namesake – as we drove miles down a dirt road astounded me. So did the array of monzogranite rocks, each looking like a restaurant-sized boulder that rises three or four stories high. There hadn't been a person in sight since leaving the main park road a few miles back.

We parked in a dirt lot, the Stress Relief rock a short walk in front of us.

When we reach it, ropes dangled down the cliff face, which looked utterly smooth.

I ran my hand across it. "We can climb this kind of rock?"

He nodded. "There are plenty of holds, and where the face is smooth there are anchors so we can hoist ourselves up."

I canted my head up, brought a hand to my forehead to block out the sun. "Looks like it's about eight stories up."

"That's about right."

He probably thinks I'm a scaredy cat, I thought. *I'll show him I can climb with the best of 'em.*

I stuck my helmet on my head, fastened its strap. "Let's do this!"

He winced then said, "Okay" and donned his helmet.

I wasn't too loud, was I?

***

I blush. "No – I couldn't have been that loud."

"You were. And you really should make amends for it."

I grin mischievously. "Yeah, how would I do that?"

He goes over to the knee-high boulder at the rock's center, sits on it. "Come over here and find out."

I pull up my panties and walk over to him, throwing a little sway into my hips, and he looks up at my face. "In addition to being extremely loud, you've been very naughty for wearing those panties while climbing this rock." He grabs my wrist and pulls me over his knees.

A squeal escapes my mouth, as I stumble onto him. His free hand breaks my fall so I don't get hurt.

He places his hand on my lower back as the other hand caresses my round butt cheeks. A moment of peace overcomes me, as my eyes close. I'd never been spanked by a guy before, just some random slaps on the butt while undressing or fucking, and I wonder what'll it be like.

"You got such a beautiful, perky little butt," he says.

Then he slowly and not too hard slaps each cheek with an open hand, his fingers flat and together.

I tense. "Ooh!"

Mario repeats the slaps, and I begin to feel the burn.

He rubs the red spots, scrubbing out the pain in them. "No one can hear us right now. That's because the slaps were light. That will soon change."

His hand brushes over the summit of my bare behind,

then begins slapping again, nonstop. I jump a little at each strike, and yelps soon morph into groans, as my bottom quivers.

Mario stops, pulls my panties down to just above the knees. The light wind soothes my roasted ass.

Then the slaps begin again, growing harder and louder, and I swear I can hear the ringing of his hand against my ass and my moans of ecstatic agony echoing off the mountain ranges.

With each smack, the heat builds, and soon I am squirming, desperate not just to protect my ass but to rub my hardened clit against his leg.

His fingers separate, and when his flat hand smacks my ass, the sting sharpens.

And then all I hear is noise – the slap of his hand on my ass, my deep and rapid breaths, my euphoric screams from the pain of his strikes and the rising wind of pleasure as my exposed clit polishes itself against his skin.

My entire body tenses and straightens, as if it were a board, then my legs kick out as I let out the loudest groan of my life. I hear it echoing from one side of the valley to the other than back again, as I slump upon his knees.

His hand soothes my throbbing ass, as quiet returns to our rock.

***

The quiet in Joshua Tree surprised me, as we donned our harnesses and connected them to the ropes. I felt like I was on one of my hikes through the wildlife sanctuary.

Mario scanned the rock face, quickly identified a handhold. His fingers dug into it then his feet went to a crack in the cliff a few inches off the ground, and he was off. His muscles rippled as he pulled himself up, foot by foot. Staring at him, a little wetness dripped onto my panties, and I decided to get going myself up the rock just to take my mind off him. Besides, maybe up top we could do a little something together, I told myself.

I spotted a fingerhold, and my hands pressed into it. The rock, at least starting out, was easy enough, and for that I felt relieved. I didn't want to embarrass myself in front of him.

Besides, if I wasn't climbing, I'd probably stand there masturbating myself as watching him climb.

***

Mario helps me to my feet then stands himself. He steps behind me, guides me so I'm facing the boulder. His hand slowly presses my upper back downward until I'm bent over the rock, my red ass and wet pussy jutting into the air. A slight breeze tickles both.

I hear him pulling down his boxers, as I plant my palms on the boulder to steady myself. He steps between my legs, and his cockhead nudges my dripping folds.

A moment later, I gasp as he enters me. My eyes close in pleasure, as he fills my pussy, igniting every nerve in its walls.

Mario grips my waist, letting me know I am his possession, that I am his to fuck. He takes me slowly, sliding in and out at a leisurely pace. Eyes closed, my head bobs up in ecstasy then down in exhaustion, as his cock claims me.

Fucking in the wide open atop the tallest rock on the horizon – no, that is hardly humdrum or boring, I tell myself. When was the last time I've done that?

Oh, that's right – *never.*

I grit my teeth, thrust back against him, urging his cock to fuck me faster. His strong grip on my waist tightens again, preventing me from moving. He is in control here, and he wants me to know that.

Gradually his thrusts quicken, and soon he's hammering into me. I groan loudly each time he fills me. The rock scratches my palms, but I don't mind, for I feel nothing but pleasure from he being inside me.

As I pant and moan all at once, he makes one last momentous thrust. His hands grip me harder, as he roars and releases his cum into me.

And then every muscle in my body tenses again, and I let go another scream as waves and waves of pleasure spin through me. My brain feels like it's on crack cocaine.

Moments later, Mario's hands loosen their hold, and my toes uncurl. He steps back.

I stand up, turn to face him. His hands are on his knees as he huffs and puffs, his cock, still fully erect, glistening in the sun from my juices. At last he stands, and I step toward him, some of his seed dripping from my pussy onto my thigh.

Mario holds his hand out for me, and I take it. He

leads me to where we were sitting before, and we slowly go to the ground, naked together. His hand caresses my face, and we kiss.

"Wow," I say, "you are one hell of a bull."

He grins. Our hawk riding the thermals returns in the distance. "I gain strength from the quiet," Mario says.

"In that case, I won't say another damn word."

My body leans into his, and this time he wraps an arm around me, holds me close. We stare out at the horizon, it moments ago filled by the sounds of our lovemaking, it now quiet and at peace, just as I am.

Just as *we* are.

Pink Tomato

"The colors you've used!"

Xavier only nodded as I a cooed over his designs. His portfolio truly was impressive – a retro peach soda can done in neon orange and purple...a logo of beige pottery on a background that I couldn't decide if it was more brown or gray...a gradient of gold to turquoise on a tube of antiperspirant.

If only he'd show as much passion toward me as he did his designs. He hadn't even noticed my short black dress and thigh-highs that evening.

I'm sure those blue eyes and that cleft chin of his had seen a fair number of short black dresses in this studio of course. But for the past few weeks, I'd been that skirt.

I closed his portfolio. "Thanks for sharing that with me. You're really quite good."

He shrugged.

I eyed him, trying to identify what he really meant by that gesture. "You know," I said at last, "sometimes I think you don't really believe my praise is worth much."

His eyes shot up. *Good, that got him feeling something.* "No, that's not what I think, Tori."

"What do I know about graphic design, after all? I'm just a barista."

He shook his head. "That's not it at all."

"What is it then?"

"I'm...I'm just tired."

"That's why you don't ever seem excited when I'm around?"

He froze. *Caught.*

"I mean, you're okay with me always coming over, but you never seem–"

Xavier placed his hands on my shoulders, focused his attention on me. *Okay, now that's some emotion.* "I love you very much. And I do value your opinion."

I let that linger in the air a moment. "Prove it."

He let go of me, looked as if he were deep in thought a moment. "Well, I am having trouble with one design."

"Oh?" Not quite what I was looking for, but I guess it was a start.

He went over to his computer, opened a file. A collage of plump ripe tomatoes appeared in various shades of pink and red. "It's for this company called Pink Tomato. I can't seem to get the right shade of pink though."

I stood next to him, real close, breathed in his scent, it like a smooth bourbon. He was right. There was carnation pink, watermelon pink, even Barbie pink, but they all looked wrong, like when some little kid colors a tree trunk orange.

"The thing is, I always think of a tomato as bright red, maybe a little darker than an apple's red. But trying to think of it as pink, well, my mind just can't wrap around it..."

"Try some pinks that are darker." I pushed another chair next to him, sat down.

He tapped several keys, shifted the mouse around, tapped yet more keys, enlarged one tomato, tapped other keys. I quietly slipped off my heels and let my toe touch his foot.

Xavier remained focused on the screen. *Time to up the ante.*

I rubbed my toe gently along his leg, just above the ankle.

He looked back at me.

I batted my eyes at him.

Xavier returned to the screen, tapped away, and I frowned. Then he asked, "Like that?"

The tomato was the color of a red tulip. "Mmm...a little lighter maybe."

He nodded, went back to the keyboard. My toe went back to his leg, slowly traced a line up to his knee. Any higher, and I'd tip over in my chair.

"Um, wait a minute," he said then reached under his seat and pulled off his shoes. *That's a good sign.*

As his attention returned to his computer, my foot massaged his then slipped up to his ankle. My sole melded around it.

Still, nothing seemed to matter to him than that computer screen. *Damn, am I going to have to get on my knees and suck his cock to get his full attention? No, he'd probably just keep typing over my head. The canvas of his screen means far more to him than I do.*

Yet for as much as he ignored me, the more I wanted him, like a cookie set out in plain sight but you have to wait until after dinner to eat. Except with Xavier, dinner might never come. *Damn it, I'm going to eat that cookie.*

My sole went up his leg.

"You're being a naughty girl," he said as typing, then he stopped and turned to me.

I gave him a playful smile.

Xavier spun his chair away from the computer toward me, then leaned in. He swept my hair over an ear and took a good look at me.

Our eyes locked onto one another, and I felt as if I could drown in the blueness of his. I hoped the sensual dip of my head and the way I lightly bit the corner of my lip would send his biology into overdrive.

If it doesn't, this will.

Standing, I reached behind my back and undid the zipper on my dress, then my fingers pulled it off my shoulders. Gravity took it to my waist, then I wiggled it down my hips and thighs until it fell to the floor below me. I stood there in my black lace bra and black thigh-highs. Oh, had I neglected to say I hadn't worn any panties that night?

Xavier's eyes widened, and I stepped right up to him. His fingers traced the curve of my hips, the touch like a flicker of wind over my bare skin. Then settling on a spot, his hands gripped me, as his head moved to my pussy. The point of his tongue licked straight up my slit, separating my folds.

"Ooooh," I murmured, as my head arched back and eyes closed.

An instant later, he found my clit, easy to do for when swollen it's pinker and larger than usual, a blessing if there ever was one given some men's cluelessness. My hands grasped the back of his head. Xavier's tongue made slow, luxurious circles, and I grinded forward. *Maybe he's not so clueless after all.* For a long moment, Xavier sucked in my labia, as I caressed his soft, black hair, then he returned to my clit, circling it slowly then ever so gradually increasing his speed, until my hips grinded in rhythm against his mouth. My breathing deepened, and his finger dipped into my pussy, then withdrew slightly and thrust in again. I let out a little whimper and bit my lips, as his hand cupped a breast, gently squeezed it, and brushed against my hardening nipple.

Every muscle in my body tightened, and then it began, that wonderful release, and I threw my head back and let out a loud gasp and for the longest moment felt as if I were floating on a current of warm air. I collapsed against Xavier, and he held me tight.

After a minute, I tried to stand, but with still weak legs and my head dizzy, I stumbled back into him.

He chuckled. "My, you are a naughty girl, aren't you?" He slapped my butt.

I jumped and yelped, but in the same instant my heart started pounding, as I felt my pussy grow wet again. And then, I was struck by the most brilliant thought.

"Say, I have an idea about that pink tomato problem you're facing."

"What?" he said.

I leaned over the chair so that my butt was on full

display for him. "The problem is your canvas."

"My canvas?"

"My complexion is the perfect canvas to find a shade of pink. Spank me and see what color you get."

For a moment he didn't move, as if contemplating whether I was serious. I wiggled my butt. "Naughty girls should be spanked, don't you agree?" I said playfully.

He rose, kneaded my lower back. "You look so sexy bent over like that. How does the massage feel?"

"Really nice," I said slowly and with eyes closed, luxuriated in his kneading. "I was wondering when you would touch me."

Xavier placed his fingertips on my butt cheeks, gazed at them for an agonizing moment as a shiver of anticipation ran through me. "And how does this feel?"

His palm slapped my ass, and I winced. Before my face could relax, he slapped it, then again, and then once more. The sting hit me like a thousand rose bush thorns brought down on my bare skin all at once.

There was a pause as he adjusted his stance, and I caught my breath. Then his hand came down hard on my other cheek, then again and again and again, as I gritted my teeth.

My breathing quickened, and nipples hardened against the constraints of my lace bra.

Then he slapped one butt cheek and then the other and repeated it over and over. My ass burned, like it were being held over a fire. One of my legs bent upward, a totally reflex action.

I was losing control to him.

And he knew it.

His strikes came down faster and harder, the stinging impact echoing off the wall, and my mouth flew open, wanting to scream, as my ass felt like it was on fire. *Surely now he sees my pussy juices slowly dripping down the inside of my thigh.*

He stopped. I could feel the heat of his stare watching it. My hand flew back to my butt, tried to rub out the pain. He pushed it away.

"It's not quite the right pink," he said, "but I think we're almost there."

His hand pressed on my lower back, and the other slapped the top of my butt, then the bottom, then each cheek, focusing on the parts that already burned, reddening them even more.

I closed my eyes, moaned.

There was one more sharp slap, and he pulled back.

"Yes, I think that it's it – that's the right color."

He quickly went over to this computer and glancing at my ass then the screen, found the matching hex code for the tomato.

I remained still, not wanting to mess with his canvas.

"What do you think of this?" he said.

I looked over my shoulder. "It's perfect!" It really was.

"You won't believe what hex color it is."

My eyes widened, as I shrugged.

"FF5470. *Fiery rose.*"

I giggled – and then he pulled his shirt over his head and unbuckled his belt, let his pants drop to the floor. His erect cock pushed the front of his boxers outward.

He tugged them down past his thighs, let them fall to the floor as well. He stepped out of the puddle of clothes, his large beige cock and its purple head bobbing with each step.

I grinned. *Finally some passion.*

If you got a little excited from reading this book, please take a few moments to write a review of it:
tinyurl.com/yckhj9ma
XOXOXO – Emily

Interview with Emily

Q: How did you come to write this collection?
A: I used to write literary and historical fiction. One topic I really wanted to explore, though, was women's sexuality, especially after reading Audre Lorde's essay *The Uses of the Erotic: The Erotic as Power.* She argued that the erotic serves as a "source of creative energy, inner power, and self-knowledge" and that each of us can harness that power to lead more authentic and fulfilling lives. I decided to write stories in which my protagonists – all women – come to realize that. I think that especially comes through in the collection's opener, "Curiouser and Curiouser."

Q: Why spanking stories and not some other fetish?
A: Probably because I'm most interested in spanking! (laughs) Most published spanking erotica stories really are about the dom and sub dynamic, while others are just male fantasies sold to women. I thought this fetish was ripe for exploration from a new perspective – the woman who wants to harness the erotic so she can be genuine and satisfied. Some women actually enjoy being spanked as part of their sexual play.

Q: Did you write the stories in the order they appear?
A: No. I arranged them in an order that I thought would best express the collection's theme. "Curiouser and Curiouser" nicely introduces the concept while "Fisherman's Eyewash" builds on it. That latter story

actually was the first written for the collection and the former story the last one I wrote!

Q: Which story was the most difficult to write?

A: Each story offered its own challenges, usually about how to get a specific scene right. "Come Hither" probably took the longest to write because I had to figure out step-by-step how Caitlynn and her best friend's father would logically end up in bed together.

Q: Do you have a favorite from the collection?

A: I like them all for different reasons, but "Fisherman's Eyewash" probably is my favorite. It's tight and punchy, and all of its sections are layered with meaning. Theme-wise, it's a great exploration of a protagonist who can't find true happiness until she accepts herself – and the perfect partner for her is the one who accepts her and patiently helps her toward that realization.

Q: Which erotica writers most inspired you?

A: My writing style probably was influenced by non-erotica writers, especially the modern classics. For erotica, I'd rank Anaïs Nin as among the best. Among current authors, Rachel Kramer Bussel stands out, as does Tiffany Reisz. Bussel is a well-known erotica editor of anthologies, and I like a lot of her story selections.

Q: Will you write more spanking stories?

A: Absolutely! I have another dozen or so already partially written. There will be plenty of other kinks and conflictful relationships I'll explore as well, from ménage à trois and younger women with older men to anal sex and coworkers who despise one another, and that's all just the tip of what I want to write about.

About Emily Rooks

Emily Rooks is the author of erotic romance that sizzles with passion and tension. Her stories explore sexuality from a woman's perspective and feature strong female protagonists. She holds a bachelor's degree in literature and creative writing and resides in Los Angeles.

True Lust Titles

Anthologies
- Backdoor Tales
- Spanking Tales
- Spanking Tales, Volume II
- Young Studs

Short Stort Standalones
- Atonement
- Chalk
- Opportunity
- Star Pupil
- Supergirl
- Venus Fly Trap

Better Sex Guidebooks
- Essential Foreplay Tips

Connect with Emily

BlueSky
emilyrookstruelust.bsky.social

Facebook
(limited posts)
facebook.com/EmilyRooksTrueLust

Goodreads
goodreads.com/user/show/146421357-emily-rooks

Literotica
literotica.com/authors/EmilyRooks/works/stories

Pinterest
pinterest.com/emilyrookstruelust

Website
emilyrookstruelust.com

X/Twitter
x.com/EmilyRooksTrueL

www.ingramcontent.com/pod-product-compliance
Lightning Source LLC
Chambersburg PA
CBHW070753120626
46557CB00002B/571